MW00438087

The

FLORAL BIRTHDAY BOOK

The
FLORAL
BIRTHDAY
BOOK:

Flowers and their Emblems,

WITH

APPROPRIATE SELECTIONS FROM THE POETS

WITH 368 ILLUSTRATIONS

Applewood Books
Carlisle, Massachusetts

Thank you for purchasing an Applewood Book.
Applewood reprints America's lively classics—books
from the past that are still of interest to modern readers.
For a free copy of our current catalog, please write to
Applewood Books, P.O. Box 27, Carlisle, MA 01741.

ISBN 978-1-55709-385-1

10

Printed in China

Library of Congress Card Number: 00-105701

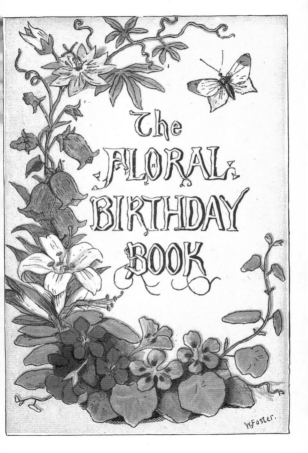

The FLORAL BIRTHDAY BOOK

W Foster.

SPAKE full well, in language quaint and olden,
    One who dwelleth by the castled Rhine,
When he call'd the flowers, so blue and golden,
    Stars that in earth's firmament do shine.

.   .   .   .   .   .

And the Poet, faithful and far-seeing,
    Sees, alike in stars and flowers, a part
Of the self-same universal being,
    Which is throbbing in his brain and heart.

Gorgeous flowerets in the sunlight shining,
    Blossoms flaunting in the eye of day,
Tremulous leaves, with soft and silver lining,
    Buds that open only to decay ;—

Brilliant hopes, all woven in gorgeous tissues,
    Flaunting gaily in the golden light ;
Large desires, with most uncertain issues,
    Tender wishes, blossoming at night !

These in flowers and men are more than seeming ;
    Workings are they of the self-same powers,
Which the Poet, in no idle dreaming,
    Seeth in himself and in the flowers.

                                      LONGFELLOW.

THE
FLORAL
BIRTHDAY BOOK

THE FLORAL BIRTHDAY BOOK

January 1.

Grass—Utility.

TRUST no Future, however pleasant,
　Let the dead Past bury its dead;
Act, act in the living Present,
　Heart within, and God o'erhead.

Lives of great men all remind us,
　We can make our lives sublime,
And, departing, leave behind us
　Footprints on the sands of Time;

Footprints, that perchance another,
　Sailing o'er Life's solemn main,
A forlorn and shipwrecked brother,
　Seeing, may take heart again.
　　　　　　　　LONGFELLOW.

Bay—Glory.

January 2.

OH! think, when a hero is sighing,
　What danger in such an adorer!
What woman could think of denying
　The hand that lays laurels before her?

No heart is so guarded around,
　But the smile of a victor would take it;
No bosom could slumber so sound,
　But the trumpet of glory will wake it!
　　　　　　　　MOORE.

Ivy—Friendship.

January 3.

Some I remember, and will ne'er forget,
My early friends, friends of my evil day,
Friends of my mirth, friends of my mi-
    sery too;
Friends given by God, in mercy and in
    love;
My counsellors, my comforters, and
    guides;
My joy in grief, my second bliss in joy;
Companions of my young desire; in
    doubt,
My oracles, my wings in high pursuit.

                  POLLOK.

Laurel—Ambition.

January 4.

He who ascends to mountain tops shall
    find
The loftiest peaks most wrapt in clouds
    and snow;
He who surpasses, or subdues, man-
    kind,
Must look down on the hate of those
    below.

                  BYRON.

Cypress—Mourning.

January 5.

Oh! lady, twine no wreath for me,
Or twine it of the cypress tree!
Too lightly grow the lilies light,
The varnish'd holly's all too bright;
The May-flower and the eglantine
May shade a brow less sad than mine;
But, lady, twine no wreath for me,
Or weave it of the cypress tree.

                  SCOTT.

January 6.

BUT when he came, though pale and
    wan,
  He looked so great and high,
So noble was his manly front,
  So calm his steadfast eye;
The rabble rout forbore to shout,
    And each man held his breath,
For well they knew the hero's soul
  Was face to face with death.

               AYTOUN.

Box—Firmness.

January 7.

LADY, you are the cruellest she alive,
If you will lead these graces to the
    grave,
And leave the world no copy.

            SHAKSPEARE.

Ice Plant—
Rejected Addresses.

January 8.

"OH ! never," she cried, "could I think
  of enshrining
An image whose looks are so joyless
  and dim ;
But yon little god upon roses reclining,
We'll make, if you please, sir, a Friendship of him."
So the bargain was struck ; with the
  little god laden,
She joyfully flew to her shrine in the
  grove :
"Farewell," said the sculptor ; "you're
  not the first maiden
Who came but for Friendship, and took
  away Love."

            MOORE.

Arbutus—
Love or Friendship.

Turnip—Charity.

January 9.

BLEST Charity ! the grace long-suffer-
    ing, kind,
Which envies not, has no self-vaunting
    mind ;
Is not puffed up, makes no unseemly
    show,
Seeks not her own, to provocation slow ;
No evil thinks, in no unrighteous choice
Takes pleasure, doth in truth rejoice ;
Hides all things, still believes, and hopes
    the best,
All things endures, averse to all contest.
                    BISHOP KEN.

Heath—Solitude.

January 10.

To climb the trackless mountain all un-
    seen,
With the wild flock, that never needs a
    fold ;
Alone, o'er steeps and foaming falls to
    lean,—
This is not solitude ; 'tis but to hold
Converse with Nature's charms, and
    view her stores unrolled.
                    BYRON.

Cresses—Stability.

January 11.

AND still his name sounds stirring
    Unto the men of Rome,
As the trumpet blast that cries to them
    To charge the Volcean home ;
And wives still pray to Juno
    For boys with hearts as bold
As his, who kept the bridge so well,
    In the brave days of old.
                    MACAULAY.

January 12.

OH, haste ! hark the shepherd
    Hath waken'd his pipe,
And led out his lambs
    Where the blae-berry's ripe :
The bright sun is tasting
    The dew on the thyme ;
Yon glad maiden's lilting
    An old bridal-rhyme.
There's joy in the heaven,
    And gladness on earth —
So come to the sunshine,
    And mix in the mirth.

ALLAN CUNNINGHAM.

Houseleek—Vivacity.

January 13.

THE angry word suppress'd, the taunt-
    ing thought ;
Subduing and subdued the petty strife
Which clouds the colour of domestic
    life ;
The sober comfort, all the peace which
    springs
From the large aggregate of little
    things,—
On these small cares of daughter, wife,
    or friend,
The almost sacred joys of home depend.

HANNAH MORE.

Sage—Domestic Virtues.

January 14.

STRANGERS yet !
Oh ! the bitter thought to scan
All the loneliness of man !—
Nature, by magnetic laws,
Circle into circle draws ;
But they only touch when met,
Never mingle—strangers yet !

LORD HOUGHTON.

Lichen—Dejection.

13

Fir—Elevation.

January 15.

. . . . . God keeps a niche
In heaven to hold our idols; and albeit
He brake them to our faces, and denied
That our close kisses should impair
     their white,
I know we shall behold them raised,
     complete,
The dust swept from their beauty,—
     glorified;
New Memnons singing in the great
     God-light.

MRS. BARRETT BROWNING.

Iceland Moss—Health.

January 16.

And though I cannot boast, O Health!
     Of aught besides, but only thee,
I would not change this bliss for wealth,
     No, not for all the eye can see.

Then hail, sweet charm! ye breezes,
     blow!
     Ransack the flower and blossom'd
     tree;
All, all your stolen gifts bestow,
     For Health has granted all to me.

CLARE.

Orange—Generosity.

January 17.

I give thee all,—I can no more
     Though poor the offering be;
My heart and lute are all the store
     That I can give to thee.

MOORE.

January 18.

Be such, and only such, my friends,
　　Once mine, and mine for ever;
And here's a hand to clasp in theirs,
　　That shall desert them never.

And thou be such, my gentle love,
　　Time, chance, the world defying;
And take—'tis all I have—a heart
　　That changes but in dying.
　　　　　　　　　　DOANE.

Cedar—Constant.

January 19.

Absent or present, still to thee,
　　My friend, what magic spells belong!
As all can tell who share, like me,
　　In turn, thy converse and thy song.

But when the dreaded hour shall come,
　　By friendship ever deemed too nigh,
And "Memory," o'er her Druid's tomb
　　Shall weep that aught of thee can die:

How fondly will she then repay
　　The homage offered at thy shrine,
And blend, while ages roll away,
　　Her name immortally with thine
　　　　　　　　　　BYRON.

*Arbor Vitæ—
Unchanging Friendship.*

January 20.

Too late for the rose the evening rain—
　　　　Mary Hamilton;
Too late for the lamb the shepherd's pain—
　　　　Mary Hamilton.
Too late at the door the maiden's stroke;
Too late for the plea when the doom hath
　　been spoke!
Too late the balm when the heart is broke—
　　　　Mary Hamilton.
　　WHYTE MELVILLE.

*Laurustinus—
"I die if neglected."*

15

Endive—Frugality.

January 21.

NEVER exceed thy income. Youth may make
    Even with the year; but age, if it will hit,
Shoots a bow shot, and lessens still his stake
    As the day lessens, and his life with it.
Thy children, kindred, friends, upon thee call:
Before thy journey, fairly part with all.

             GEORGE HERBERT.

Ilex—Endurance.

January 22.

THROUGH long days of anguish,
    And sad nights, did pain
Forge my shield, Endurance,
    Bright and free from stain.

             ADELAIDE PROCTER.

Fennel—Strength.

January 23.

ABOVE the lowly plants it towers,
The fennel, with its yellow flowers;
And in an earlier age than ours,
Was gifted with the wondrous powers,
    Lost vision to restore.

It gave new strength, and fearless mood,
And gladiators fierce and rude
Mingled it in their daily food;
And he who battled and subdued,
    A wreath of fennel wore.

             LONGFELLOW.

January 24.

Ground Ivy—Humility.

THE bird that soars on highest wing,
   Builds on the ground her lowly nest ;
And she that doth most sweetly sing,
   Sings in the shade when all things rest.
In lark, and nightingale, we see
What honour hath humility.

MONTGOMERY.

January 25.

Cineraria—A Star.

OH ! star of strength, I see thee stand,
   And smile upon my pain ;
Thou beckonest with thy mailèd hand,
   And I am strong again.

The star of the unconquered will,
   He rises in my breast,
Serene, and resolute, and still,
   And calm, and self-possessed.

LONGFELLOW.

January 26.

Thyme—Thriftiness.

OH, wasteful woman ! she who may
   On her sweet self set her own price,
Knowing he cannot choose but pay—
   How has she cheapened Paradise !
How given for nought her priceless gift,
   How spoiled the bread, and spilled the
      wine,
Which, spent with due respective thrift,
   Had made brutes men, and men divine !

COVENTRY PATMORE.

Olive—Peace.

January 27.

PEACE be around thee, wherever thou
    rovest !
  May life be for thee one summer's day ;
And all that thou wishest, and all that
    thou lovest,
  Come smiling around thy sunny way.

If sorrow e'er this calm should break,
  May even thy tears pass off so lightly,
Like spring showers, they'll only make
  The smiles that follow shine more
    brightly.

MOORE.

Stonecrop—Tranquillity.

January 28.

Now fades the glimmering landscape on
    the sight,
And all the air a solemn stillness holds,
Save where the beetle wheels her droning
    flight,
And drowsy tinklings lull the distant folds

Save that from yonder ivy-mantled tower
The moping owl does to the moon com-
    plain,
Of such as, wandering near her secret
    bower,
Molest her ancient solitary reign.

GRAY.

Truffle—Surprise.

January 29.

"CHLORIS, I swear, by all I ever swore,
  That from this hour I shall not love thee
    more."
"What ! love no more? Oh, why this
    alter'd vow ?"
"Because I *cannot* love thee *more*—
    than now."

MOORE.

January 30.

AND her against sweet Cheerfulnesse was
    placed,
Whose eyes, like twinkling stars in even-
    ing cleare,
Were deckt with smiles, and all sad
    humours chased,
And darted forth delight, the which her
    goodly graced.

SPENSER.

**Variegated Holly—
Always Cheerful.**

January 31.

THE seraph Abdiel, faithful found
Among the faithless, faithful only he ;
Among innumerable false, unmoved,
Unshaken, unseduced, unterrified,
His loyalty he kept, his love, his zeal ;
Nor number, nor example with him
    wrought,
To swerve from truth, or change his con-
    stant mind.

MILTON.

White Ivy—Rarity.

February 1.

. . . . So we grew together,
Like to a double cherry, seeming parted,
But yet a union in partition ;
Two lovely berries moulded on one stem :
So, with two seeming bodies, but one heart ;
Two of the first, like coats in heraldry,
Due but to one, and crowned with one crest.
And will you rent our ancient love asunder,
To join with men in scorning your poor
    friend ?   SHAKSPEARE.

**Chilian Pine—
"You bewilder me."**

Snowdrop—Hope.

February 2.

HAS Hope, like the bird in the story
　　That flitted from tree to tree,
With the talisman's glittering glory—
　　Has Hope been that bird to thee?

On branch after branch alighting,
　　The gem did she still display,
And when nearest and most inviting,
　　Then waft the fair gem away?

MOORE.

Champignon—Suspicion.

February 3.

"AND on!" said the youth, "since to-
　　morrow I go,
To fight in a far distant land,
Your tears for my absence soon ceasing to
　　flow,
Some other will court you, and you will be-
　　stow
On a wealthier suitor your hand."
"Oh! hush those suspicions!" fair Imo-
　　gine said,
　　"Offensive to love and to me;
For if you be living, or if you be dead,
I swear by the Virgin that none in your stead
　　Shall husband of Imogine be!"

LEWIS.

Evergreen Clematis—
Poverty.

February 4.

ALAS! that Poverty's evil eye
　　Should e'er come hither
　　Such sweets to wither!
The flowers laid down their heads to die,
And Hope fell sick as the witch drew nigh.
　　She came one morning,
　　Ere Love had warning,
And raised the latch where the young god
　　lay:
"Oh, oh!" said Love, "is it you? Good-
　　bye!"
So he opened the window, and flew away.

MOORE.

February 5.

THEY tell thee to doubt me,
  And think of me no more ;
They say I have sported
  With other hearts before :
But when you hear unkind ones speak,
With venomed tongue and smiling cheek,
  Repel them, and tell them
    That I 've been true to thee.

OLD SONG.

Crocus—Abuse not.

February 6.

O THOU, the friend of man assign'd,
With balmy hands his wounds to bind,
  And charm his frantic woe ;
When first distress, with dagger keen,
Broke forth to waste his destined scene,
  His wild unsated foe !

By Pella's bard, a magic name—
By all the griefs his thought could frame,
  Receive my humble rite :
Long, Pity, let the nation view
Thy sky-worn robes of tenderest blue,
  And eyes of dewy light.

COLLINS.

Camellia Japonica—Pity.

Prickly Pear—Satire.

February 7.

CURST be the verse, how well soe'er it
    flow,
That tends to make one worthy man my
    foe,—
Give virtue scandal, innocence a fear,
Or from the soft-eyed virgin steal a tear.

POPE.

**Almond Tree—
Indiscretion.**

February 8.

But 'tis not to list to the waterfall,
That Parisina leaves her hall ;
And it is not to gaze on the heavenly light
That the lady walks in the shadow of night
And if she sits in Este's bower ;
'Tis not for the sake of its full-blown
    flower ;
She listens—but not for the nightingale,
Though her ear expects as soft a tale.

                    BYRON.

Kalmia—Nature.

February 9.

How canst thou renounce the boundless
    store
Of charms which Nature to her votary
    yields,—
The warbling woodland, the resounding
    shore,
The pomp of groves, and garniture of fields
All that the genial ray of morning gilds,
And all that echoes to the song of even ;
All that the mountain's sheltering bosom
    yields,
And all the dread magnificence of Heaven,
Oh, how canst thou renounce, and hope to
    be forgiven ?

                    BEATTIE.

Primula—Animation.

February 10.

Lightsome, brightsome cousin mine,
Easy, breezy Caroline !
With thy locks all raven shaded,
From thy merry brow up-braided,
And thine eyes of laughter full,
    Brightsome cousin mine !
Thou in chains of love hast bound me,
Wherefore dost thou flit around me,
    Laughter-loving Caroline ?

                BON GAULTIER.

February 11.

HASTE thee, nymph, and bring with thee
Jest and youthful jollity,
Quips and cranks, and wanton wiles,
Nods, and becks, and wreathed smiles,
Such as hang on Hebe's cheek,
And love to live in dimple sleek.

MILTON.

**Spring Crocus—
Youthful Gladness.**

February 12.

AH ! were she as pitiful as she is fair,
Or but as mild as she is seeming so,
Then were my hopes greater than my
   despair,
Then all the world were heaven, nothing
   woe.

. . . .

So as she shows, she seems the budding
   rose,
Yet sweeter far than is an earthly flower ;
Sovereign of beauty, like the spray she
   grows,
Compass'd she is with thorns and can-
   kered flower ;
Yet were she willing to be pluck'd and worn,
She would be gathered though she grew
   on thorn.

ROBERT GREEN.

**Larch Fir—
Deceitful Charms.**

**Moon Daisy—
Love's Oracle.**

February 13.

Margaret.—He loves me—not—he loves
me—not—(*as she plucks off the last
leaf with eager delight*)—he loves
me !

Faust.—Yes, my child, deem this language of the flower the answer of an
oracle—" He loves thee !"

GOETHE.

**Pyrus Japonica—
Love at First Sight.**

February 14.

OH ! there are looks and tones that dart
An instant sunshine through the heart,
As if the soul that minute caught
Some treasure it through life had sought ;
As if those very lips and eyes,
Predestined to have all our sighs,
And never be forgot again,
Sparkled and spoke before us then.
So came thy every look and tone,
When first on me they breathed and shone,
New, as if brought from other spheres,
Yet welcome as if loved for years.

MOORE.

**Irish Ivy—
Clinging Affection,**

February 15.

I THINK of thee ! my thoughts do twine
  and bud
About thee, as wild vines, about a tree,
Put out broad leaves, and soon there's
  nought to see,
Except the straggling green which hides
  the wood.

MRS. BARRETT BROWNING.

**Purple Violet—
"You occupy my thoughts."**

February 16.

OH, how, or by what means may I contrive
To bring the hour that brings thee back
  more near ?
How may I teach my drooping hope to
  live
Until that blessed time, and thou art here ?
I 'll tell thee : for thy dear sake I will lay
  hold
Of all good aims, and consecrate to thee,
In worthy deeds, each moment that is told,
While thou, beloved one, art far from me.

FANNY KEMBLE.

February 17.

Awake, ye sons of Spain! awake! advance!
Lo! Chivalry, your ancient goddess, cries,
But wields not, as of old, her thirsty lance,
Nor shakes her crimson plumage in the skies:
Now on the smoke of blazing bolts she flies,
And speaks in thunder through yon engines' roar:
In every peal she calls—"Awake! arise!"
Say, is her voice more feeble than of yore,
When her war-song was heard on Andalusia's shore?

BYRON.

Daffodil—Chivalry.

February 18.

Life, believe, is not a dream
  So dark as sages say;
Oft a little morning rain
  Foretells a pleasant day.
Sometimes there are clouds of gloom,
  But these are transient all;
If the shower will make the roses bloom,
  O why lament its fall?

CHARLOTTE BRONTË.

Daisy—Cheerfulness.

February 19.

Some minds are temper'd happily, and mix'd
With such ingredients of good sense, and taste
Of what is excellent in man—they thirst
With such a zeal to be what they approve,
That no restraints can circumscribe them more
Than they themselves by choice, for wisdom's sake,
Nor can example hurt them.

COWPER.

Deodora—Self-reverence.

Arum Lily—Ardour.

February 20.

He had no breath, no being but in hers;
She was his voice; he did not speak to her,
But trembled on her words; she was his
  sight,
For his eye followed hers, and saw with
  hers,
Which coloured all his objects; he had
  ceased
To live within himself; she was his life,
The ocean to the river of his thoughts,
Which terminated all; upon a tone,
A touch of hers, his blood would ebb and
  flow,
And his cheek change tempestuously—
  his heart
Unknowing of its cause of agony.

                                    BYRON.

*Gorse—
Enduring Affection.*

February 21.

Not lightly did I love, nor lightly choose:
What'er thou losest, I will also lose;
If bride of death—being first my chosen
  bride,
I 'll await death, lingering by thy side.

                          HON. MRS. NORTON.

Reeds—Music.

February 22.

And ever against eating cares,
Lap me in soft Lydian airs,
Married to immortal verse,
Such as the melting soul may pierce,
In notes, with many a winding bout
Of linkèd sweetness long drawn out.
With wanton heed, and giddy cunning,
The melting voice through mazes running,
Untwisting all the chains that tie
The hidden soul of harmony.

                                    MILTON.

February 23.

As the ore must for ever obedient be
    found,
  By the loadstone attracted along ;
So in England you drew all the poets
    around,
  By the magical force of your song.

DR. BURNEY.

Variegated Laurel—
Attractive.

February 24.

. . . .
THERE was but one spell upon my brain,
Upon my pencil, on my strain ;
But one face to my colours came ;
My chords replied to but one name—
Lorenzo !—all seemed vowed to thee,
To passion, and to misery !

L. E. L.

Cedar Leaf—
"I live for thee."

February 25.

BUT thou, O Hope ! with eyes so fair,
What was thy delighted measure?
Still it whisper'd promised pleasure,
And bade the lovely scenes at distance
    hail !
Still would her touch the strain prolong ;
And from the rocks, the woods, the vale,
She called on Echo still through all the
    song ;
And where her sweetest theme she chose,
A soft responsive voice was heard at every
    close,
And Hope enchanted smiled, and waved
    her golden hair.

COLLINS.

Cyclamen—Hope.

Hepatica—Confidence.

February 26.

ON she went, and her maiden smile
In safety lighted her round the Green
   Isle ;
And blest for ever is she who relied
Upon Erin's honour and Erin's pride.

MOORE.

*Garden Daisy—" I share
your sentiments."*

February 27.

AND when, as how often I eagerly listen
To stories thou read'st of the dear olden
   day,
How delightful to see our eyes mutually
   glisten,
And feel that affection has sweeten'd
   the lay.
Yes, love,—and when wandering at even
   or morning,
Through forest or wild, or by waves foaming white,
I have fancied new beauties the landscape
   adorning,
Because I have seen thou wast glad in
   the sight.

MARY HOWITT.

Buttercups—Childhood.

February 28.

HAPPY those early dayes, when I
Shin'd in my angell-infancy !
Before I understood this place,
Appointed for my second race,
Or taught my soul to fancy aught
But a white, celestiall thought ;
When yet I had not walkt above
A mile or two from my first love,
And looking back, at that short space,
Could see a glimpse of his bright face.

VAUGHAN

February 29.

THY husband is thy lord, thy life, thy
    keeper,
Thy head, thy sovereign; one that cares
    for thee,
And for thy maintenance; commits his body
To painful labour, both by sea and land,
To watch the night in storms, the day in
    cold,
While thou liest warm at home, secure and
    safe;
And craves no other tribute at thy hands,
But love, fair looks, and true obedience,—
Too little payment for so great a debt.

            SHAKSPEARE.

Bullrush—Docility.

Willow—Forsaken.

March 1.

RARELY, rarely comest thou,
    Spirit of Delight;
Wherefore hast thou left me now,
    Many a day and night?
Many a weary night and day
'Tis since thou art fled away.

How shall ever one like me
    Win thee back again?
With the joyous and the free,
    Thou wilt scoff at pain.
Spirit false! thou hast forgot
All but those who heed thee not.

            SHELLEY.

**Blue Violet—
Faithfulness.**

March 2.

I AM bound by the old promise;
    What can break that golden chain?
Not even the words that you have spoken,
    Or the sharpness of my pain.

Do you think, because you fail me,
    And draw back your hand to-day,
That from out the heart I gave you,
    My strong love can fade away?

           ADELAIDE PROCTER.

Cape Jasmine— Anticipation.

March 3.

OH ! how impatience gains upon the soul,
   When the long-promised hour of joy
      draws near !
How slow the tardy moments seem to roll
   What spectres rise of inconsistent fear !
To the fond doubting heart its hopes ap-
      pear
   Too brightly fair, too sweet to realize ;
All seem but day-dreams of delight too
      dear !
   Strange hopes and fears in painful con-
      test rise,
While the scarce-trusted bliss seems but
      to cheat the eyes.

MRS. TIGHE.

Wallflower—Fidelity.

March 4.

O WOMAN ! in our hours of ease,
Uncertain, coy, and hard to please,
And variable as the shade
By the light quivering aspen made ;
When pain and anguish wring the brow,
A ministering angel thou !

SCOTT.

Garden Anemone— Forsaken.

March 5

WI' lightsome heart I pu'd a rose,
   Fu' sweet upon its thorny tree,
And my fause luver stole my rose,
   But, ah ! he left the thorn wi' me !

BURNS.

March 6.

Sport, that wrinkled Care derides,
And Laughter holding both his sides :
Come, and trip it as you go,
On the light fantastic toe.

MILTON.

March 7.

. . . . It's my honest conviction,
That my breast is a chaos of all contra-
diction :
Religious—deistic—now loyal and warm ;
Then a dagger-drawn democrat hot for
reform :
This moment a fop—that, sententious as
Titus ;
Democritus now, and anon Heraclitus :
Now laughing and pleased, like a child
with a rattle ;
Then vexed to the soul with impertinent
tattle :
Now moody and sad, now unthinking and
gay—
To all points of the compass I veer in a
day.

KIRKE WHITE.

Wild Daisy—
Indecision.

March 8.

I'll give thee fairies to attend on thee ;
And they shall fetch thee jewels from the
deep ;
And sing, while thou on pressed flowers
dost sleep :
And I will purge thy mortal grossness so,
That thou shalt like an airy spirit go.

SHAKSPEARE.

Ivy Spray—
Assiduous to please.

Kingcup—
"I wish I was rich."

March 9.

THEN why this ceaseless, vain unrest?
Earth opens her impartial breast
To prince and beggar both; nor might
Gold e'er tempt Hell's grim satellite
To waft astute Prometheus o'er
From yonder ghastly Stygian shore.
Proud Tantalus and all his race
He curbs within that rueful place;
The toil-worn wretch, who cries for ease,
Invoked or not, he hears and frees.

HORACE.

White Violet—Modesty.

March 10.

TRUE modesty is a discerning grace,
And only blushes in the proper place;
But counterfeit is blind, and skulks,
    through fear,
Where 'tis a shame to be ashamed t' ap-
    pear:
Humility the parent of the first,
The last by vanity produced and nursed.

COWPER.

Marshmallow—
Kindness.

March 11.

WHO is Sylvia? what is she,
  That all our swains commend her?
Holy, fair, and wise is she,
  The heavens such grace did lend her,
That she might admirèd be.

Is she kind as she is fair?
  For Beauty lives with kindness;
Love doth to her eyes repair,
  To help him of his blindness;
And being helped, inhabits there.

SHAKSPEARE.

March 12.

Cucumber—Criticism.

Ah ! ne'er so dire a thirst of glory boast,
Nor in the critic let the man be lost.
Good nature and good sense must ever
    join ;
To err is human, to forgive Divine.

POPE.

March 13.

Star-like her eyes—but seem'd suffused
    with woe,
As thus she spoke, in accents soft and low :
Poet ! whose fame shall reach from sea to
    sea,
Till Heaven's eternal orbs forget to roll,
Oh ! haste thee hence, and save a sinking
    soul,
Forlorn by Fortune, yet beloved by me !

. . . .

Double Daffodil—Regard.

Beatrice sends thee to the world above
(Her bosom throbbing with eternal love,
That leads her from the fount of pure de-
    light),
In mercy to oppose his mad career,
Where yonder paths to swift destruction
    bear,
She hovers on the bounds of ancient
    night.

DANTE.

March 14.

Thou sail'st with others in this Argus
    here,
No wrack or bulging thou hast cause to
    fear ;
But trust to this, my noble passenger :
Who swims with Virtue, he shall still be
    sure,
Ulysses-like, all tempests to endure,
And 'midst a thousand gulfs to be secure.

HERRICK.

Mint—Virtue.

Primrose—Youth.

March 15.

I would I were a careless child,
Still dwelling in my Highland cave,
Or roaming through the dusky wild,
Or bounding o'er the dark blue wave
                                    BYRON.

March 16.

When Love is kind,
    Cheerful and free,
Love's sure to find
    Welcome from me;
But when Love brings
    Heartache or pang,
Tears, and such things,
    Love may go hang!

                                    MOORE.

Mustard—Indifference.

March 17.

Lady, where'er you roam, whatever land
Woos the bright touches of that artist
    hand;
Whether you sketch the valley's golden
    meads,
Where mazy Linth his lingering current
    leads;
Enamour'd catch the mellow hues that sleep
At eve on Mielleries' immortal steep:
Or musing o'er the Lake, at day's decline,
Mark the last shadow on that holy shrine,
Where many a night the shade of Tell
    complains
Of Gullias' triumph, and Helvetia's chains;
Oh! lay the pencil for a moment by,
Turn from the canvas that creative eye,
And let its splendour, like the morning ray
Upon a shepherd's harp, illume my lay.

                                    MOORE.

Auricula—Painting.

34

March 18.

We twa ha' run about the braes,
    And pu'd the gowans fine;
But we've wander'd mony a weary foot
    Sin' auld lang syne.

BURNS.

Red Periwinkle—
Early Friendships.

March 19.

. . . . A hidden strength,
Which, if Heaven gave it, may be term'd
    heroism:
'Tis chastity, my brother, chastity:
She that has that, is clad in complete
    steel,
And, like a quiver'd nymph with arrows
    keen,
May trace huge forests, and unharbour'd
    heaths,
Infamous, and sandy perilous wilds,
Where, through the sacred rays of chastity
No savage fierce, bandit, or mountaineer,
Will dare to soil her virgin purity.

MILTON.

Orange Blossom—Chastity.

Blue Hyacinth—Constancy

March 20.

It is not while beauty and youth are thine
    own,
    And thy cheek unprofaned by a tear,
That the fervour and faith of a soul can be
    known,
    To which Time will but make thee more
    dear.

MOORE.

Rhubarb—Advice.

March 21.

Do not trust him, gentle lady,
  Though his voice be low and sweet;
Heed not him who kneels before thee,
  Gently pleading at thy feet.

COARD.

Garden Ranunculus—
"You are rich in attraction."

March 22.

THEY tell me thou'rt the favoured guest
Of every fair and brilliant throng,—
No wit like thine to wake the jest,
No voice like thine to breathe the song.

MOORE.

Orchis—A Beauty.

March 23.

ON her fair cheeks' unfading hue,
The young pomegranate's blossoms strew
Their bloom in blushes ever new;
Her hair in hyacinthine flow,
Then left to roll its folds below,
(As 'midst her handmaids in the hall
She stood superior to them all,)
Hath swept the marble where her feet
Gleamed whiter than the mountain sleet,
Ere from the cloud that gave it birth
It fell, and caught one stain of earth.

BYRON.

March 24.

Wild Violet—
Love in Idleness.

YET mark'd I where the bolt of Cupid fell:
It fell upon a little Western flower,
Before milk-white, now purple with Love's
wound,
And maidens call it Love in Idleness.

SHAKSPEARE.

March 25,

Lenten Lily—
Reciprocal Love.

No one is so accursed by fate,
No one so utterly desolate,
But some heart, though unknown,
Responds unto his own,—

Responds, as if with unseen wings
An angel touch'd its quivering strings,
And whispers in its song,
Where hast thou stayed so long?

LONGFELLOW

March 26.

Double Daisy—Participation.

YET once again, but once before we sever,
    Fill we the brimming cup—it is the last;
And let these lips, now parting, and for
    ever,
    Breathe o'er this pledge the memory of
    the past!

MRS. KEMBLE.

Peppermint—Cordiality.

March 27.

THE broken soldier, kindly bade to stay,
Sat by his fire, and talk'd the night away,
Wept o'er his wounds, or, tales of sorrow
    done,
Shoulder'd his crutch, and show'd how
    fields were won.
Pleased with his guests, the good man
    learn'd to glow,
And quite forgot their vices in their woe;
Careless their merits or their faults to scan,
His pity gave, ere charity began

GOLDSMITH.

White Periwinkle—
Pleasant Recollections.

March 28.

OFT in my waking dreams do I
    Live o'er again that happy hour,
When midway on the mount I lay,
    Beside the ruined tower.

The moonshine stealing o'er the scene,
    Had blended with the light of eve;
And *she* was there, my hope, my joy,
    My own dear Genevieve.

COLERIDGE.

Heartsease—Thoughts.

March 29

SAID he—"I would dream for ever, like
    the flowing of that river,
Flowing ever in a shadow greenly onward
    to the sea!
So, thou vision of all sweetness, princely
    to a full completeness,
Would my heart and life flow onward,
    deathward, through this dream of *thee*."

MRS. BARRETT BROWNING.

March 30.

Evening Primrose—Inconstancy.

SIGH no more, ladies, sigh no more;
 Men were deceivers ever,
One foot on sea, and one on shore,
 To one thing constant never.
  Then sigh not so,
  But let them go,
 And be you blithe and bonny;
Converting all your sounds of woe
 Into, hey nonny, nonny!

      SHAKSPEARE.

March 31.

Polyanthus—Pride of Riches.

WEALTH, and the high estate of pride,
With what untimely speed they glide,
  How soon depart!
Bid not the shadowy phantoms stay;
The vassals of a mistress they,
  Of fickle heart.

These gifts in Fortune's hands are found;
Her swift revolving wheel turns round,
  And they are gone!
No rest th' inconstant goddess knows,
But changing, and without repose,
  Still hurries on.

      LONGFELLOW.

April 1.

Palm—Victory.

FAREWELL, ye vanishing flowers, that shone
 In my fairy wreath, so bright and brief;
Oh! what are the brightest that e'er have blown,
I'o the lote-tree springing by Allah's throne,
 Whose flowers have a soul in every leaf?
Joy, joy for ever! my task is done—
The gates are pass'd, and Heaven is won.

      MOORE.

Purple Hyacinth—Sorrow.

April 2.

I, WHO was Fancy's lord, am Fancy's slave,
　Like the low murmurs of the Indian
　　shell,
Ta'en from its coral bed beneath the wave,
　Which, unforgetful of the ocean's swell,
Retains within its mystic urn the hum
　　Heard in the sea grots where the Ne-
　　reids dwell:
Old thoughts still haunt me—unawares
　　they come
　Between me and my rest, nor can I make
Those aged visitors of sorrow dumb.

AYTOUN.

Cowslip—Pensiveness.

April 3.

SUN of the sleepless! melancholy star!
Whose tearful beam shows tremulously far,
That show'st the larkness thou canst not
　　dispel,—
How like art thou to joy remember'd well!
So gleams the past, the light of other days,
Which shines, but warms not, with its
　　powerless rays.
O! nightbeam sorrow watcheth to behold,
Distinct, but distant, clear, but, oh! how
　　cold!

BYRON.

Wood Anemone—Sickness.

April 4.

IF music be the food of love, play on;
Give me excess of it: that surfeiting,
The appetite may sicken, and so die.

SHAKSPEARE.

April 5.

WHAT means this tumult in a Vestal's
  veins?
Why rove my thoughts beyond this last
  retreat?
Why feels my heart its long-forgotten heat?
Yet, yet, I love! From Abelard it came;
An Eloisa yet must kiss the name.
Dear, fatal name! rest ever unreveal'd,
Nor pass these lips in holy silence seal'd:
Hide it, my heart, within that close dis-
  guise,
Where, mixed with God's, his loved idea
  lies.

POPE.

Crimson Polyanthus—
The Heart's Mystery.

April 6.

SWEET flower! that with thy soft blue eye,
  Didst once look up in shady spot,
To whisper to the passer-by
  Those tender words, "Forget-me-not!"

Thou speak'st of hours when I was young,
  And happiness arose unsought:
When she, the whispering woods among,
  Gave me thy bloom, Forget-me-not!

BON GAULTIER.

Garden Forget-me-not.
"Forget me not."

April 7.

To you my soul's affections move,
  Devoutly, warmly true;
My life has been a task of love,
  One long, long thought of you.

If all your tender faith be o'er,
  If still my truth you'll try,
Alas! I know but one proof more—
  I'll bless your name, and die!

MOORE.

Pear Tree—Affection.

Saffron Crocus—Mirth.

April 8.

AND in thy right hand lead with thee
The mountain nymph, sweet Liberty ;
And if I give the honour due,
Mirth, admit me of thy crew,
To live with her, and live with thee,
In unreproved pleasures free.

MILTON.

Lilac Polyanthus—
Confidence in Heaven.

April 9.

TELL me not, in mournful numbers,
　　Life is but an empty dream ;
For the soul is dead that slumbers,
　　And things are not what they seem.

Life is real ! life is earnest !
　　And the grave is not its goal ;
" Dust thou art, to dust returnest,"
　　Was not spoken of the soul.

LONGFELLOW.

Globe Ranunculus—" I am
dazzled by your charms."

April 10.

THY every look, and every grace,
　　So charm whene'er I view thee,
Till death o'ertake me in the chase,
　　Still will my hopes pursue thee.

Then, when my tedious hours are past,
　　Be this last blessing given—
Low at thy feet to breathe my last,
　　And die in sight of Heaven !

WILLIAM HAMILTON.

April 11.

Ah me! full sorely is my heart forlorn,
To think how modest worth neglected lies,
While partial Fame doth with her blasts
    adorn
Such deeds alone as pride and pomp dis-
    guise—
Deeds of ill sort, and mischievous emprise.
Lend me thy clarion, goddess! let me try
To sound the praise of merit ere it dies;
Such as I oft have chancèd to espy,
Lost in the shades of dull obscurity.
SHENSTON.

Red Primrose—
Unpatronised Merit.

April 12.

And I bend the knee before her,
    As a captive ought to bow:
Pray thee, listen to my pleading,
    Sovereign of my soul art thou!

Oh, my dear and gentle lady,
    Let me show thee all my pain,
Ere the words that late were prisoned
    Sink into my heart again.
AYTOUN.

Peach Blossom—
"I am your captive."

April 13.

But if for me thou dost forsake
Some other maid, and rudely break
Her worshipp'd image from its base,
To give to me the ruin'd place;—

Then fare thee well! I'd rather make
My bower upon some icy lake,
When thawing suns begin to shine,
Than trust to love so false as thine!
MOORE.

Apricot Blossom—Doubt.

43

Marjoram—Blushes.

April 14.

IN everlasting blushes seen,
Such Pringle shines, of sprightly mien ;
To her the power of love imparts—
Rich gift !—the soft successful arts
That best the lover's fire provoke,—
The lively step, the mirthful joke,
The speaking glance, the amorous wile,
The sportful laugh, the winning smile.
Her soul awakening every grace,
Is all abroad upon her face :
In bloom ot youth still to survive,
All charms are there, and all alive.

WILLIAM HAMILTON.

Wild Ranunculus— Inconstancy.

April 15.

ONE year ago my path was green,
My footstep light, my brow serene ;
Alas ! and could it have been so,
      One year ago ?

There is a love that is to last,
When the hot days of youth are past ;
Such love did a sweet maid bestow,
      One year ago.

I took a leaflet from her braid,
And gave it to another maid :
Love ! broken should have been thy bow,
      One year ago.

SAVAGE LANDOR.

Cherry Tree—Education.

April 16.

A LITTLE learning is a dangerous thing ;
Drink deep, or taste not the Pierian spring ;
There shallow draughts intoxicate the brain,
And drinking largely sobers us again.

POPE.

April 17.

"Oh, stay! I cried, "bright vision, stay,
  And leave me not forlorn!"
But smiling still they passed away,
  Like shadows of the morn.

One spirit still remained, and cried,
  "Thy soul shall ne'er forget!"
He standeth ever by my side,
  The phantom call'd Regret.

ADELAIDE PROCTER.

Wistaria—Regret.

April 18.

Lesbia wears a robe of gold,
  But all so close the nymph hath laced it,
Not a charm of Beauty's mould
  Presumes to stay where Nature placed it.
Oh! my Nora's gown for me,
  That floats as wild as mountain breezes,
Leaving every beauty free
  To sink or swell as Heaven pleases.
Yes, my Nora Creina, dear—
Nature's dress is loveliness
  The dress you wear, my Nora Creina.

MOORE.

Sweetbriar—Simplicity.

April 19.

You smile to see me turn and speak
  With one whose converse you despise;
You do not see the dreams of old
  That with his voice arise;
How can you tell what links have made
  Him sacred in my eyes?

Oh! there are voices of the past,
  Links of a broken chain,
Wings that can bear me back to times
  Which cannot come again;
Yet God forbid that I should lose
  The echoes that remain.

ADELAIDE PROCTER.

Tendrils of Climbing
Plants—Links.

**Blue Periwinkle—
Pleasures of Memory.**

April 20.

So the bells of Memory's wonder city
    Peal for me their old melodious chime;
So my heart pours forth a changeful ditty,
    Sad and pleasant from the bygone time.

Domes and towers and castles, fancy
    builded,
    There lie lost to daylight's garish beams,
There lie hidden, till unveiled and gilded,
    Glory gilded, by my nightly dreams.
        From the German of MULLER.

Wood Sorrel—Joy.

April 21.

THE clouds are at play in the azure space,
And their shadows at play on the bright
    green vale;
And here they stretch to the frolic chase,
And there they roll on the easy gale.
There's a dance of leaves in that aspen
    bower,
There's a titter of winds in that beechen tree,
There's a smile on the fruit, and a smile on
    the flower,
And a laugh from the brook that runs to
    the sea.
And look at the broad-faced sun, how he
    smiles
On the dewy earth, that smiles in his ray,
On the leaping waters, and gay young isles
Aye, look, and he'll smile thy gloom away.
        BRYANT.

**Red Tulip—
Declaration of Love.**

April 22.

I TOLD her how he pined; and, ah!
    The deep, the low, the pleading tone
With which I sang another's love
    Interpreted my own.
        COLERIDGE.

April 23.

HALF my life is full of sorrow,
    Half of joy still fresh and new ;
One of these lives is a fancy,
    But the other one is true.

. . . .

Which, you ask me, is the real life?
    Which the dream—the joy, or woe?
Hush, friend ! it is little matter,
    And, indeed—I never know.

                    ADELAIDE PROCTER.

Shamrock—Joy in Sorrow.

April 24.

As by the shore, at break of day,
A vanquish'd chief expiring lay,
Upon the sands, with broken sword,
He traced his farewell to the free ;
And there the last unfinish'd word
He dying wrote, was "Liberty!"

At night a sea-bird shriek'd the knell
Of him who thus for Freedom fell ;
The words he wrote, ere evening came,
Were covered by the sounding sea :
So pass away the cause and name
Of him who dies for Liberty !

                    MOORE.

Water Willow— Freedom.

April 25.

I LIVE among the cold, the false,
    And I must seem like them ;
And much I am, for I am false
    As these I most condemn :
I teach my lip its sweetest smile,
    My tongue its softest tone ;
I borrow others' likeness, till
    I almost lose my own.

                    CHANDLER.

White Cherry Tree—
Deception.

47

American Cowslip—
"You are my Divinity."

Larch—Daring.

Amaranth—Immortality.

April 26.

WHAT scenes appear where'er I turn my
    view!
The dear ideas, where I fly, pursue,
Rise in the grove, before the altar rise,
Stain all my soul, and wanton in my eyes.
I waste the matin lamp in sighs for thee;
Thy image steals between my God and me;
Thy voice I seem in every hymn to hear,
With every bead I drop too soft a tear.
When from the censer clouds of fragrance
    roll,
And swelling organs lift the rising soul,
One thought of thee puts all the pomp to
    flight—
Priests, tapers, temples, swim before my
    sight.

                POPE.

April 27.

I LOOKED upon his brow—no sign
    Of guilt or fear was there;
He stood as proud by that death-shrine,
    As even o'er despair
He had a power; in his eye
    There was a quenchless energy,
      A spirit that could dare
The deadliest form that death could take,
And dare it for the daring's sake.

                L. E. L.

April 28.

NEVER here, for ever there,
Free from parting, pain, and care,
Where Death and Time shall disappear
For ever *there*, but *never here*.
The timepiece of Eternity
Sayeth this incessantly—
    For ever! Never! Never! For ever!

              LONGFELLOW.

April 29.

Happy when we but seek to endure
A little pain, then find a cure,
　　By double joy requited;
For friendship, like a sever'd bone,
Improves, and gains a stronger tone,
　　When aptly reunited.

COWPER.

*Weeping Willow—
Melancholy.*

April 30.

Go!—you may call it madness, folly,
　　You shall not chase my gloom away;
There's such a charm in melancholy,
　　I would not, if I could, be gay.

O! if you knew the pensive pleasure
　　That fills my bosom when I sigh,
You would not rob me of a treasure
　　Monarchs are too poor to buy.

ROGERS.

*Forget-me-not—
"Forget me not."*

May 1.

I hardly know one flower that blows
　　On my small garden plot;
Perhaps I may have seen a *rose*,
　　And said, *Forget-me-not.*

SAVAGE LANDOR.

Saffron—Marriage.

May 2.

But earthly happier is the rose distilled,
Than that which, withering on the virgin
   thorn,
Grows, *lives*, and *dies* in single blessed-
   ness.

SHAKSPEARE.

May 3.

There be more things to greet the heart
   and eyes
In Arno's Dome of Arts, most princely
   shrine,
Where Sculpture with her rainbow sister
   vies;
There be more marvels yet—but not for
   mine;
For I have been accustomed to entwine
My thoughts with Nature rather in the
   fields,
Than Art in galleries: though a work
   divine
Calls for my spirit's homage, yet it yields
Less than it feels, because the weapon
   which it wields
Is of another temper.

BYRON.

Acanthus—The Fine Arts.

*Virginian Creeper—
Sweet Neglect.*

May 4.

Give me a look, give me a face,
T'at makes simplicity a grace;
Robes loosely flowing, hair as free:
Such sweet neglect more taketh me,
Than all th' adulteries of art;
They strike mine eyes, but not my heart.

BEN JONSON

May 5.

No walls were yet, nor fence, nor moat,
    nor mound,
Nor drum was heard, nor trumpet's angry
    sound ;
Nor swords were forged ; but, void of care
    and crime,
The soft Creation slept away their time.
The flowers unseen in field and meadows
    reigned,
And western winds immortal Spring
    maintained ;
From veins of valleys milk and nectar
    broke,
And honey sweating through the pores of
    oak.

OVID.

Beech Tree—Prosperity.

May 6.

Joy is the mainspring in the whole
    Of endless Nature's calm rotation ;
Joy moves the dazzling wheels that roll
    In the great timepiece of Creation :
Joy breathes on buds, and flowers they
    are ;
    Joy beckons—suns come forth from
        heaven ;
Joy rolls the spheres in realms afar ;
    Ne'er to thy glass, dim Wisdom, given.

SCHILLER.

Celandine—Joy.

May 7.

COME, my own heart !—none reads too oft
    himself !
Can all the stars this outward earth illume?
E'en day itself leaves half our orb in gloom :
But one lone lamp lights up the spirit's
    vault —
The egotist has wisdom in his fault.

BULWER LYTTON.

Narcissus—Egotism.

Black Thorn—Difficulty.

May 8.

THE brightest gems in heaven that glow,
  Shine out from midmost sky;
The whitest pearls of the sea below,
  In its lowest caverns lie.

He must stretch afar, who would reach a
    star,
  Dive deep for the pearl, I trow;
And the fairest rose that in Scotland blows,
  Hangs high on the topmost bough.

WHYTE MELVILLE

Apple Blossom—Choice.

May 9.

. . . . A COTTAGE snug and neat,
Upon the top of many-fountain'd Ide,
That I might thence, in holy fervour, greet
The bright-gown'd morning tripping up
    her side;
And when the low sun's glory-buskin'd
    feet
Walk on the blue wave of the Ægean tide,
Oh! I would kneel me down and worship
    there
The God who garnish'd out a world so
    bright and fair.

TENNANT.

Flowering Fern—Meditation.

May 10.

LIKE the low murmur of the secret stream,
Which through dark alders winds its
    shaded way,
My suppliant voice is heard: ah! do not
    deem
That on vain toys I throw my hours away.

In the recesses of the forest vale,
On the wild mountain, on the verdant sod,
Where the fresh breezes of the morn prevail,
I wander lonely, communing with God.

AIRD.

May 11.

Oh! even while he leapt, his horrid thought
Was of the peril to that lady brought;
Oh! even while he leapt, her Claud look'd
    back,
And shook his hand to warn her from the
    track.
In vain : the pleasant voice she loved so
    well
Feebly re-echoed through that dreadful
    dell,—
The voice that was the music of her home
Shouted in vain across that torrent's foam.
He saw her pausing on the bank above;
Saw—like a dreadful vision of his love—
That dazzling dream stand on the edge of
    death.

HON. MRS. NORTON.

Rhododendron—Danger.

Elm—Dignity.

May 12.

Grace was in all her steps, heaven in
    her eye,
In every gesture dignity and love.

MILTON.

Lilac (Purple)—
First Emotions of Love.

May 13.

Oh! who would not welcome that mo-
    ment's returning,
    When Passion first waked a new life
    through his frame,
And his soul—like the wood that grows
    precious in burning—
    Gave out all its sweets to Love's ex-
    quisite flame.

MOORE.

Harebell—Grief.

May 14.

So, you see, my life is twofold.
    Half a pleasure, half a grief;
Thus all joy is somewhat temper'd,
    And all sorrow finds relief.

ADELAIDE PROCTER.

Chesnut—Do me Justice.

May 15.

SPEAK of me as I am: nothing extenu-
    ate,
Nor set down aught in malice. Then
    must you speak
Of one, that loved not wisely, but too
    well;
Of one not easily jealous, but, being
    wrought,
Perplex'd in the extreme: of one whose
    hand,
Like the base Judean, threw a pearl
    away,
Richer than all his tribe; of one whose
    subdu'd eyes,
Albeit unused to the melting mood,
Dropt tears as fast as the Arabian trees
Their medicinal gum. Set you down this.

SHAKSPEARE.

Water=Lily—Invocation.

May 16.

    SABRINA fair,
Listen, where thou art sitting
Under the glassy, cool, translucent wave,
In twisted braids of lilies knitting
The loose train of thy amber-dropping
    hair;
Listen, for dear Honor's sake,
Goddess of the silver lake,—
    Listen, and save!

MILTON.

May 17.

Hawthorn—Hope.

HOPE comes again, to this heart long a
    stranger,
Once more she sings me her flattering
    strain ;
But hush, gentle syren ! for all, there's
    less danger
In suffering on, than in hoping again.

                 MOORE.

May 18.

. . . . . WHAT could I do?
Cot, garden, vineyard, and wood,
Lake, sky, and mountain, went along with
    him !
Could I remain behind ? . . . .
. . . . I followed him

Maiden-hair Fern—Secrecy.

To Mantua ! To breathe the air he
    breathed,
To walk upon the ground he walk'd upon,
To look upon the things he look'd upon,
To look, perchance, on him !—perchance
    to hear him—
To touch him !—never to be known to him,
Till he was told, I lived and died his love !

        SHERIDAN KNOWLES.

May 19.

Syringa—Memory.

SLIGHT withal may be the things which
    bring
Back on the heart the weight which it
    would fling
Aside for ever : it may be a sound,
A tone of music—summer's eve, or spring—
A flower—the wind—the ocean, which shall
    wound,
Striking the electric chain wherewith we're
    darkly bound.

           BYRON.

Elder—Mercy.

May 20.

ONCE, staggering, blind with folly, on the
    brink of hell,
Above the everlasting fire-flood's frightful
    roar,
God threw his heart before my feet, and,
    stumbling o'er
That obstacle Divine, I into heaven fell.

ORIENTAL.

Osier—Candour.

May 21.

HIS nature is too noble for the world;
He would not flatter Neptune for his
    trident,
Or Jove for his power to thunder.   His
    heart's his mouth:
What his breast forges, that his tongue
    must vent.

SHAKSPEARE.

Laburnum—Forsaken.

May 22.

WHY didst thou praise my humble charms,
    And, oh! then leave them to decay?
Why didst thou win me to thy arms,
    Then leave me to mourn the livelong
    day?

The village maidens of the plain
    Salute me lowly as they go,
Envious they mark my silken train,
    Nor think a Countess can have woe.

MICKI E.

May 23.

RIVER of all my hopes, thou wert and art,
The current of thy being bears my heart;
Whether it sweep along in sh`ne or shade,
By barren rocks, or banks in flowers ar-
    rayed,
Foam with the storm, or glide in soft
    repose.—
In that deep channel, Love unswerving
    flows.

            HON. MRS. NORTON.

Bluebell—Constancy.

May 24.

LOOK, nymphs and shepherds, look!
What sudden blaze of majesty
Is that we from hence descry,
Too divine to be mistook?
    This, this is she
To whom our vows and wishes bend;
Here our solemn search hath end.

Fame, that, her high worth to raise,
Seem'd erst so lavish and profuse,
We may justly now accuse
Of detraction from her praise;
Less than half we find exprest,
Envy bid conceal the rest.

            MILTON.

**First Rose of Summer—
Majesty.**

May 25.

THE world goes up, and the world goes
    down,
  And sunshine follows the rain;
And yesterday's sneer and yesterday's
    frown
  Can never come over again,
    Sweet wife,—
  No, never come over again.

            CHARLES KINGSLEY.

Pimpernel—Change.

**Lily of the Valley—
Return of Happiness.**

May 26.

THEN a mighty gush of passion
　Through my inmost being ran;
Then my older life was ended,
　And a dearer course began.

Dearer!—oh, I cannot tell thee
　What a load was swept away,—
What a world of doubt and darkness
　Faded in the dawning day.

AYTOUN.

Poplar—Courage.

May 27.

BUT now he stood, cha'ned and alone,
　The headsman by his side,
The plume, the helm, the charger gone;
　The sword which had defied
The mightiest, lay broken near;
　And yet no sign, no sound of fear,
Came from that lip of pride;
And never king or conqueror's brow
Wore higher look than his did now.

L. E. L.

**Red Tulip—
Confession of Love.**

May 28.

LOVE thee?—so well, so tenderly,
　Thou'rt loved, adored, by me,
Fame, fortune, wealth, and liberty,
　Are worthless without thee!

MOORE.

May 29.

BLEST be that spot, where cheerful guests
    retire
To pause from toil, and trim their evening
    fire ;
Blest that abode, where want and pain
    repair,
And every stranger finds a ready chair.
Blest be those feasts, with simple plenty
    crown'd,
Where all the ruddy family around
Laugh at the jests or pranks, that never
    fail,
Or sigh with pity at some mournful tale,
Or press the bashful stranger to his food,
And learn the luxury of doing good.
GOLDSMITH.

Oak—Hospitality.

May 30.

SOMETIMES, with secure delight,
    The upland hamlets will invite,
    When the merry bells ring round,
    And the jocund rebecks sound,
To many a youth, and many a maid,
Dancing in the chequer'd shade.
MILTON.

Sothernwood—Merriment.

May 31.

FAME is the spur that the clear spirit doth
    raise
(That last infirmity of noble minds)
To scorn delights, and live laborious days ;
But the fair guerdon when we hope to find,
And think to burst out into sudden blaze,
Comes the blind Fury with th' abhorrèd
    shears,
And slits the thin-spun life.
MILTON.

Tulip Tree—Fame.

Rose (Gloire de Dijon)—
Gladness.

June 1.

But never yet, by night or day,
In dew of spring, or summer's ray,
Did the sweet Valley shine so gay
As now it shines, all love and light,
Visions by day, and feasts by night!
A happier smile illumes each brow,
    With quicker spread each heart uncloses,
And all is ecstacy,—for now
    The Valley holds its Feast of Roses.
                                MOORE.

June 2.

Rose (Daily)—
"Welcome me."

So a fresh and glad emotion
    Rose within my swelling breast,
And I hurried swiftly onwards,
    To the haven of my rest.

Thou wert there with word and welcome,
    With thy smile so purely sweet;
And I laid my heart before thee,
    Laid it, darling, at thy feet,
                                AYTOUN.

June 3.

Rose (Cabbage)—
Ambassador.

"Go, gentle Muse! and when my anthems
        rise,
Where Heaven's loud chorus charms the
        list'ning skies,
One thankful strain shall yet remember
        thee!"
She ceased; and thus her wish my answer
        crown'd:
"Prompt at thy will, and to thy orders
        bound,
Thy faithful delegate, thy servant, see!
Spirit benign! whose disentangled soul
Thy brethren taught to spurn the nether
        goal,
Pierce the blue mundane shell, and claim
        the sky;
Such energy attends thy warm request,
That my strong wish outruns my winged
        haste,
Nor need you more your holy influence
        try."   DANTE.

June 4.

Rose (Bridal)—Happy Love.

. . . . . WHEN we love,
All air breathes music, like the branchy
    bower,
By Indian bards feign'd, which, with
    ceaseless song,
Answers the sun's bright raylets; nor till
    eve
Folds her melodious leaves, and all night
    rests,
Drinking deep draughts of silence.

BAILEY.

June 5.

**Rose (Austrian)—
"Thou art all that is lovely."**

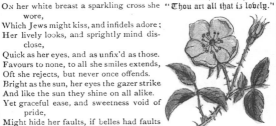

On her white breast a sparkling cross she
    wore,
Which Jews might kiss, and infidels adore;
Her lively looks, and sprightly mind dis-
    close,
Quick as her eyes, and as unfix'd as those.
Favours to none, to all she smiles extends,
Oft she rejects, but never once offends.
Bright as the sun, her eyes the gazer strike
And like the sun they shine on all alike.
Yet graceful ease, and sweetness void of
    pride,
Might hide her faults, if belles had faults
    to hide;
If to her share some female errors fall,
Look in her face, and you'll forget them
    all.

POPE.

**Rose (Burgundy)—
Unconsciousness.**

June 6.

See virgin Eve, with graces bland,
    Fresh blooming from her Maker's hand,
        In Orient beauty beam!
Fair on the river-margin laid,
    She knew not that her image made
        The angel in the stream.

LOGAN.

Rose (Unique)—Modesty.

June 7.

WHETHER joy danced in her dark eye,
Or woe or pity claim'd a sigh,
Or filial love was glowing there,
Or meek devotion pour'd a prayer,
Or tale of injury call'd forth
Th' indignant spirit of the North,—
One only passion unreveal'd.
With maiden pride, the maid conceal'd,
Yet not less purely felt the flame ;—
Oh ! need I tell that passion's name ?

SCOTT.

**Rose (Caroline)—
Love is dangerous.**

June 8.

OH ! fair as the sea-flower close to thee
    growing,
    How light was thy heart till Love's
        witchery came,
Like the wind of the south o'er a summer
    lute blowing,
    And hush'd all its music, and wither'd
        its frame !
But long upon Araby's green sunny high-
    lands
    Shall maids and their lovers remember
        the doom
Of her, who lies sleeping among the pearl
    islands,
    With nought but the sea-star to light
        up her tomb.   MOORE.

**Rosebud (White)—
A Heart ignorant of Love.**

June 9.

UNTUTOR'D by science, a stranger to fear
    And rude as the rocks where my infancy
        grew,
No feeling save one to my bosom was dear
    Need I say, my sweet Mary, 'twas cen-
        ter'd in you ?
Yet it could not be love, for I knew not
    the name—
    What passion can dwell in the heart of
        a child ?
But still I perceive an emotion the same
    As I felt when a boy, on the crag-
        cover'd wild.   BYRON.

June 10.

Rose (Red-leaved)—Beauty.

BEAUTY is but a vain and doubtful good,
A shining gloss that fadeth suddenly ;
A flower that dies when first it 'gins to
    bud ;
A brittle glass that's broken presently :
A doubtful good, a gloss, a glass, a flower,
Lost, faded, broken, dead within an hour !

SHAKSPEARE.

June 11.

Rose (China)—Grace.

THEY seem'd all fair,—but there was one,
On whom the light had not yet shone,
Or shone but partly ; so downcast
She held her brow as slow she pass'd.
And yet to me there seem'd to dwell
About that unseen face—
A something in the shade that fell
Over that brow's imagined grace—
Which won me more than all the best
Outshining beauties of the rest.

MOORE.

June 12.

Rose (Dundee Rambler)—
"Only deserve my love."

"TELL me my fate !" he cried, seizing her
    hand ;
"Thy fate ?" she answered, "tell me rather
    mine !
Bend pride's stiff knees ; no longer grace
    withstand,
And I will be for ever, ever thine !
If not, then Heaven hath this dear bounty
    bann'd,
And my poor heart must thy rich heart
    resign.
I am Madonna's child, come life what
    may ;
Come death—O ! Godfrid, kneel with me,
    and pray !"

AUSTIN.

63

Rose (Deep Red)—
Bashfulness.

June 13.

COME, thou whose thoughts as limpid
    streams are clear,
To lead the train—sweet Modesty, appear!
Here make thy court, amidst our rural
    scene,
And shepherd girls shall own thee for their
    Queen.

COLLINS.

June 14.

ASK me not how much I love thee—
    Do not question why;
        I have told thee the tale,
        In the evening pale,
    With a tear and a sigh.

I told thee when love was hopeless,
    But now he is wild, and sings,
        That the stars above
        Shine ever on love,
    Though they frown on the fate of kings.

Oh, a king would have loved and left thee,
    And away thy sweet love cast;
        But I am thine,
        Whilst the stars shall shine—
    To the last—to the last!

BARRY CORNWALL.

Rosebud (Moss)—
Confession of Love.

June 15.

WELL had he learn'd to curb the crowd,
By arts that veil, and oft preserve the
    proud:
His was the lofty port, the distant mien,
That seems to shun the sight—and awes,
    if seen;
The solemn aspect, and the high-born eye,
That checks low mirth, but lacks not
    courtesy.

SCOTT.

Rose (Gloire de Santenay)—
Pride.

June 16.

Rose (Moss)—
Superior Merit.

. . . . OVERTASKED at length.
Both Love and Hope beneath the load
    give way ;
Then, with a statue's smile, a statue's
    strength,
Stands the mute sister, Patience, nothing
    loth,
And both supporting, does the work of
    both.

COLERIDGE.

June 17.

Rose (Japan)—Compassion.

FAREWELL, farewell ! but this I tell
    To thee, thou wedding guest :
He prayeth well, who loveth well
    Both man, and bird, and beast.

He prayeth best, who loveth best
    All things, both great and small ;
For the dear God who loveth us,
    He made and loveth all

COLERIDGE.

June 18.

Rose (Lancaster)—Union.

THIS—this shall be a consecrated spot ;
But *thou*—when all that birth and beauty
    throws
Of magic round thee is extinct—shall have
One-half the laurel that oe'rshades my
    grave.
No power in death can tear our names
    apart,
As none in life could rend thee from my
    heart.
Yes, Leonora ! it shall be our fate
To be entwined for ever—but too late !

BYRON.

Cluster Rose:—
"You are charming."

June 19.

When fix'd in Memory's mirror dwells
  Some dear-loved form, to fleet no more,
Transformed, as by Arabian spells,
  We catch the likeness we adore :
Then, ah ! who would not love most true ?
Who would not be in love with you ?

KEBLE.

Rose (Musk)—
A Capricious Beauty.

June 20.

When Gracia, beautiful but faithless fair,
  Who long in passion's bonds my heart
    had kept,
First with false blushes pitied my despair,
  I smiled with pleasure !—should I not
    have wept ?

And when, to gratify some wealthier wight,
  She left to grief the heart she had be-
    guiled,
The heart grew sick, and, saddening at
    the sight,
  I wept with sorrow !—should I not have
    smiled ?

MONCRIEFF.

Rosebud (Red) – "You are
young and beautiful."

June 21.

Maiden with the meek brown eyes,
In whose orbs a shadow lies,
Like the dusk in evening skies ;
Thou whose locks outshine the sun,
Golden tresses wreathed in one,
As the braided streamlets run !
Standing with reluctant feet,
Where the brook and river meet,
Womanhood and childhood fleet.

LONGFELLOW.

June 22.

CALL back the dew
  That on the rose at morn was lying;
When the day is dying,
  Bid the sunbeam stay;
Call back the wave,
  E'en while the ebbing tide's receding;
Oh! all unheeding
  Of thy voice are they!
As vain the call
  Distraction makes on love departed;
When the broken-hearted
  Bitter tears let fall.
Dew and sunshine, wave and flower,
Renewed, return at destined hour;
But never yet was known the power,
  Could vanish'd love recall.

CHARLES DICKENS.

**Rose (Yellow)—
Departure of Love.**

June 23.

Is it, O man, with such discordant noises,
  With such accursed instruments as these,
Thou drownest Nature's sweet and kindly
      voices,
  And jarrest the celestial harmonies?

Were half the power that fills the world
      with terror,
  Were half the wealth bestow'd on camps
      and courts,
Given to redeem the human mind from
      error,
  There were no need of arsenals nor forts.

LONGFELLOW.

Rose (York)—War.

June 24.

How can we live so far apart?
  Oh! why not rather, heart to heart,
    United live and die?
Like those sweet birds, that fly together,
  With feather always touching feather,
    Link'd by a hook and eye!

MOORE.

**Rose (White and Red)—
Unity.**

Rose (Damask)—Freshness.

June 25.

HER form was as the morning's blight-
    some star,
  That, capp'd with lustrous coronet of
    beams,
Rides up the dawning orient in her car,
  New wash'd, and doubly 'fulgent from
    the streams.
The Caldee shepherd eyes her light afar,
  And on his knees adores her as she
    gleams:
So shone the stately form of Maggie
    Lauder,
And so the admiring crowds pay homage
  and applaud her.   TENNANT.

Rose (Mundi)—Variety.

June 26.

AGE cannot wither her, nor custom stale
Her infinite variety.

            SHAKSPEARE.

Ask what prevailing, pleasing power
  Allures the sportive, wandering bee
To roam untired from flower to flower;
  He'll tell you, 'tis variety.

Look Nature round, her features trace,
  Her seasons, all her changes see;
And own, upon Creation's face
  The greatest charm 's variety.

            MOORE.

June 27.

LADY, do not heed her warning;
  Trust me, thou shalt find me true;
Constant as the light of morning
  I will ever be to you.

Lady, I will not deceive thee,
  Fill thy guileless heart with woe;
Trust me, lady, and believe me,
  Sorrow thou shalt never know.

            MANAHAN.

Rose (White)—
"I am worthy of you."

June 28.

. . . . . It were all one,
That I should love a bright particular star,
And think to wed it. He is so above me,
In his bright radiance and collateral light
Must I be comforted, not in his sphere.
The ambition in my love thus plagues itself:
The hind that would be mated with the lion
Must die for love.

SHAKSPEARE.

Rose (Maiden Blush)—
Timid Love.

June 29.

To kneel at many a shrine,
    Yet lay the heart on none;
To think all other charms divine,
    But those we just have won;—
This is love, faithless love,
Such as kindleth hearts that rove.

MOORE.

Rose (White Withered)—
Transient Impressions.

June 30.

So dear to Heaven is saintly chastity,
That when a soul is found sincerely so,
A thousand liveried angels lacquey her,
Driving far off each thing of sin and guilt,
And in clear dream, and solemn vision,
Tell her of things, that no gross ear can hear;
Till oft converse with heavenly habitants,
Begin to cast a beam on th'outward shape,
The unpolluted temple of the mind,
And turns it by degrees to the soul's essence,
Till all be made immortal.

MILTON.

Crown of Roses—
Reward of Chastity.

Pink—Boldness.

July 1.

Young Henry was as brave a youth
　As ever graced a martial story;
And Jane was fair as lovely truth:
　She sigh'd for Love, and he for Glory.

With her his faith he meant to plight,
　And told her many a gallant story;
Till war, their coming joys to blight,
　Call'd him away from Love to Glory.

Young Henry met the foe with pride,
　Jane followed, fought—ah! hapless
　　　story!—
In man's attire, by Henry's side;
　She died for Love, and he for Glory.

DIBDIN.

White Lily—Purity.

July 2.

Fair girl! by whose simplicity
　My spirit has been won
From the stern earthliness of life,
　As shadows flee the sun;

I turn again to think of thee,
　And half deplore the thought,
That for one instant o'er my soul
　Forgetfulness hath wrought!

I turn to that charm'd hour of hope,
　When first upon my view
Came the pure sunshine of thine heart,
　Borne from thine eyes of blue.

WILLIS CLARKE.

Sweet Pea—Departure.

July 3.

Adieu, adieu! my native land
　Fades o'er the waters blue;
The night-winds sigh, the breakers roar,
　And shrieks the wild sea-mew.

Yon sun that sets upon the sea,
　We follow in his flight;
Farewell awhile to him and thee:
　My native land—good-night!

BYRON.

July 4.

ALAS! the love of women! it is known
  To be a lovely and a fearful thing;
For all of theirs upon that die is thrown,
  And if 'tis lost, life has no more to
    bring
To them, but mockeries of the past alone.

BYRON.

July 5.

BUT if ye saw that which no eyes **can** see,
The inward beauty of her lively sp'rit,
Garnish'd with heavenly gifts of high de-
  gree,
Much more would ye wonder at that sight,
And stand astonish'd, like to those which
  r_al
Medusa's mazeful head.
There dwells sweet love and constant
  chastity,
Unspotted faith, and comely womanhood,
Regard of honour, and mild modesty;
There Virtue reigns as queen on royal
  throne,
  And giveth laws alone,
The which the base affection do obey,
And yield their services unto her will.

SPENSER.

Mignonette—Excellence.

Iris—"I have a message
for you."

July 6.

  Go, blushing flower!
And tell her this from me,
  That in the bower
From which I gathered thee,
At evening I will be.

PETER SPENCER.

Imperial Lily—Dignity.

July 7.

Lo ! she cometh in her beauty,
    Stately, with a Juno grace,
Raven locks, Madonna-braided,
    O'er her sweet and blushing face ;

Eyes of deepest violet, beaming
    With the love that knows not shame ;
Lips that thrill my inmost being,
    With the utterance of a name !

AYTOUN.

Verbena—Enchantment.

July 8.

MINE is the charm whose mystic sway
The spirits of past delight obey ;
Let but the tuneful talisman sound,
And they come like genii hovering round.
And mine is the gentle song, that bears
From soul to soul the wishes of love ;
As a bird, that wafts through genial airs
The cinnamon seed from grove to grove.
'Tis I that mingle, in one sweet measure,
The past, the present, and future of plea-
    sure.

MOORE.

Guelder Rose—
Growing Old.

July 9.

A MIRTHFUL man he was—the snows of
    age
Fell, but they did not chill him : gaiety,
Even in life's closing, touch'd his teeming
    brain,
With such visions as the setting sun
Raises in front of some hoar glacier,
Painting the bleak ice with a thousand
    hues.

SCOTT.

July 10.

WHEN slumber first unclouds my brain,
  And thought is free.
And sense, refresh'd, renews her reign,—
  I think of thee.

When, next, in prayer to God above
  I bend my knee,
Then, when I pray for those I love,—
  I pray for thee.

In short, one only wish I have—
  To live for thee ;
Or gladly, if one pang 'twould save,
  I'd die for thee.

ANON.

**Red Double Pink—
Ardent Love.**

July 11.

IT is a flame, an ardour of the mind,
Dead in the proper corpse, quick in an-
  other's ;
Transfers the lover into the loved.
That he or she that loves, engraves or
  stamps
The idea of what they love, first in them-
  selves ;
Or like to glasses, so their minds take in
The forms of their beloved, and them
  reflect.
It is the likeness of affections.

BEN JONSON.

Acacia—Chaste Love.

July 12.

GIVE me more love, or more disdain .
  The torrid or the frozen zone
Bring equal ease unto my pain—
  The temperate affords me none.
Either extreme of love or hate,
Is sweeter than a calm estate.

CAREW.

**Striped Carnation—
Extremes.**

Scarlet Geranium—Comfort.

July 13.

HAST thou found naught within thy
    troubled life,
        Save inward strife?
Hast thou found all he promised thee
    deceit,
        And hope a cheat?
Endure,—and there shall dawn within thy
    heart
        Eternal rest.   YOUNG.

July 14.

*Lotus Flower—
Estranged Love.*

"FAITHLESS Paris! cruel Paris!"
    Thus the poor deserted spake—
"Wherefore thus so strangely leave me?
    Why thy loving bride forsake?
Why no tender word at parting—
    Why no kiss, no farewell take?
Would that I could but forget thee!
    Would this throbbing heart might break

. . . .

Thou may'st find another maiden,
    With a fairer face than mine—
With a gayer voice and sweeter,
    And a spirit liker thine.
For, if ere my beauty bound thee,
    Lost and broken is the spell;
But thou canst not find another
    That will love thee half so well."
                 AYTOUN.

July 15.

Day Lily—Coquetry.

SHE who only finds her self-esteem
In others' admiration, begs an alms:
Depends on others for her daily food,
And is the very servant of her slaves;
Though oftentimes, in a fantastic hour,
O'er men she might a childish power exert,
Which not ennobles, but degrades her state.
               JOANNA BAILLIE.

July 16.

Lotus—Eloquence.

THE charms of eloquence—the skill
　To wake each secret string,
And from the bosom's chords at will
　Life's mournful music bring;
The o'ermast'ring strength of mind which
　sways
　The haughty and the free,
Whose might earth's mightiest ones obey—
　This charm was given to—thee.

MRS. EMBURY.

July 17.

Magnolia—Love of Nature.

PLEASANT were many scenes; but most
　to me,
The solitude of vast extent, untouched
By hand of art, where Nature sowed her-
　self,
And reaped her crops; whose garments
　were the clouds;
Whose minstrels brooks, whose lamps the
　moon and stars;
Whose organ choir the voice of many
　waters;
Whose banquets morning dews; whose
　heroes storms;
Whose warriors mighty winds; whose
　lovers, flowers;
Whose orators the thunderbolts of God;
Whose palaces the everlasting hills;
Whose ceiling heaven's unfathomable
　blue.

POLLOK.

July 18.

Pencil-leaved Geranium—
Genius.

BRIGHT as the pillar rose at Heaven's
　command,
When Israel march'd along the desert land,
Blazed through the night on lonely wilds
　afar,
And told the path—a never-setting star:
So, heavenly Genius, in thy course divine,
Hope is the star, her light is ever thine.

CAMPBELL.

75

**Convolvulus—
Extinguished Hope.**

July 19.

At morn, beside yon summer sea,
   Young Hope and Love reclined ;
But scarce had noon-tide come, when he
Into his bark leap'd smilingly,
   And left poor Hope behind.

"I go," said Love, "to sail awhile
   Across this sunny main :"
And then, so sweet his parting smile,
That Hope, who never dreamt of guile,
   Believed he'd come again.

. . . .

Now fast around the sea and shore
   Night threw her darkling chain ;
The sunny sails were seen no more,
Hope's morning dreams of bliss were o'er—
   Love never came again.

MOORE.

**White Jasmine—
Extreme Amiability.**

July 20.

What shall we call it, folly or good nature?
So soft, so simple, and so kind a creature?
When Charity so blindly plays its part,
It only shows the weakness of her heart.

TERENCE.

Yellow Lily—Falsehood.

July 21.

False World, thou ly'st : thou canst not lend
   The least delight ;
Thy favours cannot gain a friend,
   They are so slight ;
Thy morning pleasures make an end,
   To please at night :
Poor are the arts that thou supply'st,
And yet thou vaunt'st, and yet thou vy'st
With Heaven : fond Earth, thou boasts ;
   false World, thou ly'st.

QUARLES.

July 22.

Larkspur—Brightness.

Oh! my love has an eye of the softest blue,
    Yet it was not that that won me;
But a bright little drop from the soul was
    there,
    'Tis *that* that has undone me.
I might have forgotten that red, red lip—
    Yet how from the thought to sever?
But there was a smile from the sunshine
    within,
    And that smile I'll remember for ever.
                    WOLFE.

July 23.

French Honeysuckle—
Rustic Beauty.

Thoughtless of beauty, she was Beauty's
    self,
Recluse among the close embowering
    woods;
As in the hollow breast of Appenine,
Beneath the shelter of encircling hills,
A myrtle rises far from human eyes,
And breathes its balmy fragrance o'er the
    wild;
So flourish'd, blooming and unseen by all,
The sweet Lavinia.
                  THOMSON.

July 24.

Balsam—Impatience.

How oft my guardian angel gently cried,
  " Soul, from thy casement look, and thou
    shalt see
How he persists to knock and wait for
    thee."
    And oh! how often to that voice of
    sorrow,
" To-morrow we will open," I replied;
And when the morrow came, I answered
    still, "To-morrow!"
                  VEGA.

Yellow Carnation—Disdain.

July 25.

No tears, Celia, now shall win
    My resolved heart to return ;
I have search'd thy soul within,
    And find nought but pride and scorn.
I have learn'd thy arts, and now
Can disdain as much as thou.
Some power, in my revenge, convey
That love to her I cast away.

CAREW.

July 26.

White Pink—"You are fair and fascinating."

Her face was as the summer cloud, whereon
The dawning sun delights to rest his rays ;
Compared with it, old Sharon's vale, o'er-
    grown
With flaunting roses, had resign'd its praise.
. . . .
Her locks, apparent tufts of wiry gold,
Lay on her lily temples, fairly dangling ;
And on each hair, so harmless to behold,
A lover's soul hung mercilessly strangling ;
The piping silly zephyrs vied to enfold
The tresses in their arms so slim and
    tangling,
And thrid in sport these lover-noosing
    snares,
And played at hide-and-seek amid the
    golden hairs.

TENNANT.

July 27.

Passion Flower—Belief.

So long thy power hath blest me, sure it still
    will lead me on,
O'er moor and fen, o'er crag and torrent, till
    the night is gone ;
And with the morn those angel faces
    smile,
Which I have loved long since, and lost
    awhile.

NEWMAN.

July 28.

"O Love !" said I, in thoughtless mood,
　As deep I drank of Lethe's stream,
" Be all my sorrows in this flood
　Forgotten, like a vanish'd dream !"

But who could bear that gloomy blank,
　Where joy was lost, as well as pain ?
Quickly of Memory's fount I drank,
　And brought the past all back again ;

And said, " O Love ! whate'er my lot,
　Still let this soul to thee be true,—
Rather than have one bliss forgot,
　Be all my pains remember'd too !"

MOORE.

July 29.

THERE is a love, which is not the love only
Of the thoughtless and the young ; there
　is a love which sees
Not with the eye, which hears not with
The ears ; but in which soul is enamoured
Of soul : it is a love only high
And noble natures can conceive,—it hath
　nothing
In common with the sympathies and ties
Of coarse affection.

BULWER LYTTON.

Acacia (Rose)—
Platonic Love.

July 30.

Ho ! all who labour, all who strive,
　Ye wield a lofty power ;
Do with your might, do with your strength,
　Fill every golden hour :
The glorious privilege, to do,
　Is man's most noble dower !
Oh, to your birthright and yourselves,
　To your own souls be true !
A weary, wretched life is theirs,
　Who have no work to do.

ORME.

Bee Orchis—Industry.

79

Mountain Pink—Ambition.

July 31.

I NEVER loved ambitiously to climb,
Or trust my hand too far into the fire.
To be in heaven, sure, is a blessed thing:
But, Atlas-like, to prop heaven on one's
back,
Cannot but be more labour than delight.
Such is the state of men in honour placed
They are gold vessels made for servile
uses;
High trees, that keep the weather from
low houses,
But cannot shield the tempest from them-
selves.

NASH.

Corn—Riches.

August 1.

Can gold calm passion, or make reason
shine?
Can we dig peace or wisdom from the
mine?
Wisdom to gold prefer, for 'tis much less
To make our fortune than our happiness:
That happiness which great ones see,
With rage and wonder in a low degree,
Themselves unbless'd: the poor are only
poor,
But what are they who droop amid their
store?
Nothing is meaner than a wretch of state;
The happy only are the truly great."

YOUNG.

**Field Red Poppy—
Consolation.**

August 2.

O AWAY! my thoughts are earthward!
Not asleep, my love, art thou!
Dwelling in the land of glory
With the saints and angels now.

Brighter, fairer far than living,
With no trace of woe or pain,
Robed in everlasting beauty,
Shall I see thee once again,

By the light that never fadeth,
Underneath eternal skies,
When the dawn of Resurrection
Breaks o'er deathless Paradise.

AYTOUN.

August 3.

FULL on the casement shone the wintry
    moon,
And threw warm gules on Madeline's fair
    breast,
As down she knelt for Heaven's grace
    and boon;
Rose-bloom fell on her hands, together
    press'd,
And on her silver cross soft amethyst,
And on her hair a glory like a saint:
She seem'd a splendid angel newly drest,
Save wings, for Heaven:—Porphyro grew
    faint !
She knelt, so pure a thing, so free from
    mortal taint.

                 KEATS.

Corn Flower—Purity.

August 4.

WARM curtain'd was the little bed,
Soft pillow'd was the little head;
"The storm will wake the child," they said:
        Miserere Domine !

Cowering among the pillows white,
He prays, his blue eyes dim with fright:
"Father, save those at sea to-night !"—
        Miserere Domine !

The morning shone, all clear and gay,
On a ship at anchor in the bay,
And on a little child at play,—
        Gloria tibi, Domine !
    ADELAIDE PROCTER.

Traveller's Joy—Safety.

August 5.

I PANT for the music which is divine,
  My heart in its thirst is a dying flower;
Pour forth the sound like enchanted wine,
  Loosen the notes in a silver shower:
Like a herbless plain for the gentle rain,
I gasp, I faint, till they wake again.

Let me drink of the spirit of that sweet
    sound—
  More, O, more ! I am thirsting yet;
It loosens the serpent which care has bound
  Upon my heart, to stifle it ;
The dissolving strain, through every vein,
Passes into my heart and brain.

             SHELLEY.

Oats—Music.

Wheat—Prosperity.

August 6.

ELYSIUM shall be thine; the blissful plains
Of utmost earth, where Rhadamanthus
reigns;
Joys ever young, unmix'd with pain or fear,
Fill the wide circle of th' eternal year.
Stern Winter smiles in that auspicious clime,
The fields are florid with unfading prime;
From the bleak pole no winds inclement
blow,
Mould the round hail, or flake the fleecy
snow;
But from the breezy deep the blest inhale
The fragrant murmur of the western gale.

POPE'S HOMER.

White Poppy—Sleep.

August 7.

COME, gentle Sleep! attend thy votary's
prayer,
And, though Death's image, to my couch
repair:
How sweet, though lifeless, yet with life
to lie;
And without dying, oh, how sweet to die!

THOMAS WARTON.

Pink Geranium—Partiality.

August 8.

BE kind and courteous to this gentleman,
Hop in his walks, and gambol in his eyes;
Feed him with apricots and dewberries,
With purple grapes, green figs, and mul-
berries;
The honey-bags steal from the humble bees,
And for night tapers crop their waxen
thighs,
And light them at the fiery glowworm's
eyes,
To have my love to bed, and to arise;
And pluck the wings of painted butterflies,
To fan the moonbeams from his sleeping
eyes. SHAKSPEARE.

August 9.

. . . . HE is in love with an ideal ;
A creature of his own imagination ;
A child of air ; an echo of his heart ;
And, like a lily on a river floating,
She floats upon the river of his thoughts
                              LONGFELLOW.

Yellow Jasmine—
Grace and Elegance.

August 10.

THE maiden paused, as if again
She thought to hear the distant strain ;
With head upraised, and look intent,
And eye and ear attentive bent,
And locks flung back, and lips apart,
Like monument of Grecian art ;
In listening mood she seem'd to stand,
The guardian Naiad of the strand :
And ne'er did Grecian chisel trace
A nymph, a Naiad, or a grace,
Of finer form or lovelier face.
                              SCOTT.

Oak-leaved Geranium—
"Lady, deign to smile."

August 11.

THOU wert still the Lady Flora,
  In the morning garb of bloom :
Where thou wert was light and glory,
  Where thou wert not, dearth and gloom.

So for many days I follow'd,
  For a long and weary while,
Ere my heart rose up to bless thee,
  For the yielding of a smile.
                              AYTOUN.

Broom—Humility.

August 12.

*F*ROM a dark cloud a drop of rain
   Was falling, when, alas! ashamed
As it approach'd the boundless main,
   In woful accents it exclaim'd:
"How wide! how vast! ah me, forlorn!
   With *that* compared, I am but naught!'
While thus it view'd itself with scorn,
   A shell it in its bosom caught;
Thus conscious of its humble state,
   'Twas changed into a brilliant gem—
An orient pearl—and raised by fate
   To deck the brightest diadem.

ORIENTAL.

Indian Double Pink—
Always Lovely.

August 13.

THAT grace and elegance, so rarely seen;
That voice, which in the inmost soul is felt;
That air inspired, *t*hat heavenly gait and
   mien;
Those eyes, whose glance the proudest
   heart can melt;
Her words, where mind, and thought, and
   genius shine;
Her silence sweet, her manners all divine.

PETRARCH.

Peony—Anger.

August 14.

THEN from Olympian tops, in wrath,
Apollo took his downward path;
Well closed and fit his quiver hung,
And as like night he swept along,
The darts upon his shoulders rang,
The silver bow gave deadly clang.
He sat him from the ships apart,
Then issued forth the bitter dart;
Fleet dogs and mules at first he slew,
And next upon the men he drew;
And, as he shot, unnumber'd fires
Stream'd upwards from the funeral pyres.

POPE'S HOMER.

August 15.

But, O my first, O my best, I could not
  choose but love thee ;
O, to be a wild white bird, and seek thy
  rocky bed !
From my breast I'd give thee burial,
  pluck the down, and spread above thee ;
I would sit and sing thy requiem on the
  mountain head.
Fare thee well, my love of loves ! would I
  had died before thee !
O, to be at least a cloud, that near thee I
  might flow—
Solemnly approach the mountain, weep
  away my being o'er thee,
And veil thy breast with icicles, and thy
  brow with snow.

JEAN INGELOW.

Asphodel—"My regrets
follow you to the grave."

August 16.

. . . .

Then wilt thou remember what now
  seems to pass
Like the moonlight on water, the breath-
  stain on glass ;
O, maiden the lovely and youthful ! to
  thee
How rose-touch'd the page of thy future
  must be !   L. E. L.

Coral Honeysuckle—
"The colour of my fate."

August 17.

O maiden fair ! O maiden fair !
  How faithless is thy bosom—
To love me in prosperity
And leave me in adversity !
O maiden fair ! O maiden fair !
  How faithless is thy bosom !

The nightingale, the nightingale
  Thou tak'st for thine example :
So long as summer laughs she sings,
But in the autumn spreads her wings :
The nightingale, the nightingale
  Thou tak'st for thine example.

LONGFELLOW.

Pink Larkspur—Fickleness.

Quaking Grass—Agitation.

August 18.

LIKE one who, some imagined peril near,
Feels his warm wishes chill'd by wintry
        fear,
    And resolution sicken at the view:
Thus I perceived my sinking spirits fail,
Thus trembling I survey'd the gloomy vale,
    As near the moment of decision drew.

DANTE.

Snapdragon—Presumption.

August 19.

Is man more just than God? is man more
        pure
Than He who deems even seraphs in-
        secure!
Creatures of clay—vain dwellers in the
        dust!
The moth survives you, and are ye more
        just?
Things of a day! you wither ere the night,
Heedless and blind to Wisdom's wasted
        light!   BYRON.

Stock—Promptitude.

August 20.

ANOTHER nymph, amongst the many fair
That made my softer hours their solemn
        care,
Before the rest affected still to stand,
And watch'd my eye, preventing my com-
        mand.
Abra—she so was call'd—did soonest haste
To grace my presence; Abra went the last.
Abra was ready ere I call'd her name;
And though I call'd another, Abra came.

PRIOR.

August 21.

THERE *was* a time when bliss
Shone o'er thy heart from every look of his;
When but to see him, hear him, breathe
    the air
In which he dwelt, was thy soul's fondest
    prayer;
When round him hung such a perpetual
    spell,
Whate'er he did, none ever did so well.
Too happy days! when, if he touch'd a
    flower
Or gem of thine, 'twas sacred from that
    hour!

MOORE.

Heliotrope—Devotion.

August 22.

THE heart that has truly loved never for-
    gets,
    But as truly loves on to the close,
As the sunflower turns to her god, when
    he sets,
    The same look that she gave when he
    rose.

MOORE.

Sunflower—Adoration.

August 23.

No real Poet ever wove in numbers
    All his dream; but the diviner part,
Hidden from all the world, spake to him
    only,
    In the voiceless silence of his heart.

So with Love; for Love and Art united
    Are twin mysteries—different, yet the
    same:
Poor indeed would be the love of any,
    Who could find its full and perfect
    name.

ADELAIDE PROCTER.

Honey-flower—
Love sweet and silent.

August 24.

Virginian Jasmine—
Separation.

ALAS! they had been friends in youth,
But whispering tongues can poison truth;
And constancy lives in realms above,
And life is thorny, and youth is vain;
And to be wroth with one we love,
Doth work like madness in the brain.

COLERIDGE.

August 25.

. . . . I CANNOT flatter; I do defy
The tongues of soothers; but a braver
place
In my heart's love, hath no man than
yourself.

SHAKSPEARE.

Venus's Looking-glass—
Flattery.

SWEET, sweet is flattery to mortal ears;
And if I drink thy praise too greedily,
My fault I'll match with grosser instances:
Do not the royal souls that van the world
Hunger for praise? does not the hero burn
To blow his triumphs in the trumpet's
mouth?
And do not poets' brows throb feverous,
Till they are cool'd with laurels?

SMITH.

August 26.

UNTIL I loved I was alone:
I asked too much of intellect and grace,
To pine, though young, for every pretty
face,
Whose passing brightness to quick fancies
made
A sort of sunshine in the idle shade;
Beauties who starr'd the earth like com-
mon flowers,
The careless eglantines of wayside bowers.
I lingered till some blossom rich and rare
Hung like a glory on the scented air,
Enamouring at once the heart and eye,
So that I paused, and could not pass it by;
Then woke the passionate love within my
heart,
And only with my life shall that depart.

HON. MRS. NORTON.

Clematis—Mental Beauty.

August 27.

THEN, is the past so gloomy now,
  That it may never bear
The open smile of Nature's brow,
  Or meet the sunny air?

I know not that—but joy is power,
  However short it last;
And joy befits the present hour,
  If sadness fits the past.

AYTOUN.

Red Dahlia—Joy.

August 28.

THE time I've lost in wooing,
  In watching and pursuing
    The light that lies
    In woman's eyes,
Has been my heart's undoing.

Though Wisdom oft has sought me,
I scorn'd the lore she brought me
    My only books
    Were woman's looks,
And folly's all they've taught me.

MOORE.

Pomegranate—Folly.

August 29.

YE see yon birkie, ca'd a lord,
  Wha struts, and stares, and a' that;
Though hundreds worship at his word,
  He's but a coof for a' that.
For a' that, and a' that,
The man of independent mind,
  He looks and laughs at a' that.

BURNS.

Borage—Bluntness.

**Camomile—
Energy in Adversity.**

August 30.

THE wise and active conquer difficulties,
By daring to attempt them; Sloth, and
    Folly
Shiver and shrink at sight of toil and
    hazard,
And make the impossibility they fear.

ROWE.

**Monthly Honeysuckle—
Bond of Love.**

August 31.

I BRING thee, love, a golden chain,
  I bring thee, too, a flowery wreath.
. . . .
The chain is form'd of golden threads,
  Bright as Minerva's yellow hair,
When the last beam of evening sheds
  Its calm and sober lustre there.

The wreath of brightest myrtle wove,
  With sun-lit drops of bliss among it,
And many a rose-leaf cull'd by love,
  To heal his lip when bees have stung it.
Come, tell me which the tie shall be,
To bind thy gentle heart to me?

MOORE.

Apple—Temptation.

September 1.

WHERE your soul is tempted
  Most to trust your fate,
Then with double caution
  Linger, fear, and wait.

ADELAIDE PROCTER.

September 2.

Aloe—Sorrow.

Has sorrow thy young days shaded,
　As clouds o'er the morning fleet?
Too fast have those young days faded,
　That even in sorrow were sweet!
Does Time with his cold wing wither
　Each feeling that once was dear?—
Then, child of misfortune, come hither;
　I 'll weep with thee tear for tear.

MOORE.

September 3.

Geranium (White)—
Refinement.

In peasant life he might have known
As fair a face, as sweet a tone;
But village notes could ne'er supply
That rich and varied melody;
And ne'er in cottage maid was seen
The easy dignity of mien,
Claiming respect, yet waiving state,
That marks the daughters of the great.

SCOTT.

September 4.

Mountain Ash—Intellect.

Yet not by fetter nor by spear
　His sovereignty was held or won;
Feared—but alone as freemen fear,
　Loved—but as freemen love alone;
He waved the sceptre o'er his kind
By Nature's first great title—mind!

CROLY.

China-Aster—Variety.

September 5.

AMARYLLIS I did woo,
And I courted Phyllis too!
Daphne for her love I chose,
Chloris for that damask rose
In her cheek, I held so dear—
Yea, a thousand liked, well near,
And, in love with all together,
Fearèd the enjoying either;
'Cause, to be of one possess'd,
Barr'd the hope of all the rest.

WITHER.

Berry Wreath—Reward.

September 6.

AND he gave the monks his treasures,
Gave them all, with this behest:
They should feed the birds at noontide
Daily on his place of rest.

Saying, "From these wandering minstrels
I have learned the art of song;
Let me now repay the lessons
They have taught so well and long."

Thus the Bard of Love departed;
And, fulfilling his desire,
On his tomb the birds were feasted
By the children of the choir.

LONGFELLOW

Nut Tree—Amusement.

September 7.

WITH her book, and her voice, and her lyre,
To wing all her moments at home;
And with scenes that new rapture inspire,
As oft as it suits her to roam;
She will have just the life she prefers,
With little to hope or to fear;
And ours would be pleasant as hers,
Might we view her enjoying it here.

COWPER.

September 8.

THERE is a joy, when hearts that beat to-
gether
Sit under blossoming trees, when spring is
new;
There is a joy in summer's sultry weather,
When leafy boughs bend over lovers true.
There is a joy, deep in the autumn heather
To crouch with one who's all the world to
you;
And joy there is, 'mid winter nights and
storms,
When gleams the firelight on two happy
forms.

AUSTIN.

Nutmeg Geranium—
An Expected Meeting.

Double China-Aster—
Reciprocity.

September 9.

OFT when, oppress'd with sad foreboding
gloom,
I sat reclined upon our favourite tomb,
I've seen those sympathetic eyes o'erflow
With kind compassion for thy comrade's
woe;
Or, when less mournful subjects form'd
our themes,
We tried a thousand fond romantic
schemes;
Oft hast thou sworn, in frienship's sooth-
ing tone,
Whatever wish was mine, must be thine
own.

BYRON.

Balm of Gilead—Relief.

September 10.

I PLEDGE you in this cup of grief,
Where floats the fennel's bitter leaf!
The battle of our life is brief:
The alarm—the struggle—the relief—
Then sleep we side by side.

LONGFELLOW.

Silver-leaved Geranium—Retrospection.

September 11.

When the bright stars came out last night,
    And the dew lay on the flowers,
I had a vision of delight,
    A dream of bygone hours:

Those hours that came and fled so fast,
    Of pleasure or of pain,
As phantoms rose from out the past
    Before my eyes again.

With beating heart did I behold
    A train of joyous hours,
Lit with the radiant light of old,
    And smiling crown'd with flowers.

ADELAIDE PROCTER.

Birch Tree—Meekness.

September 12.

Give me your hand; here let me kneel:
Make your reproaches sharp as steel;
Spurn me, and smite me on each cheek—
No violence can harm the meek.

LONGFELLOW.

Dew Plant—A Serenade.

September 13.

I rise from dreams of thee,
    In the first sweet sleep of night,
When the winds are breathing low,
    And the stars are shining bright:

I rise from dreams of thee;
    And a spirit in my feet
Has led me—who knows how?—
    To thy chamber window, sweet!

SHELLEY.

September 14.

SHE gazed upon a world she scarcely knew,
  As seeking not to know it ; silent, lone,
As grows a flower, thus quietly she grew,
  And kept her heart serene within its
    zone.
There was awe in the homage which she
    drew ;
Her spirit seem'd as seated on a throne,
Apart from the surrounding world, and
    strong
  In its own strength—most strange in one
    so young

                              BYRON.

Dahlia—
Elegance and Dignity

Single China-Aster—
Indecision.

September 15.

" FAIN would I climb, but that I fear to
    fall."—
" If thy heart fail thee, climb not at all."
           SIR WALTER RALEIGH AND
                QUEEN ELIZABETH.

Daphne—Ornament.

September 16.

THEN first were diamonds from the night
Of earth's deep centre brought to light
And made to grace the conquering way
Of proud young Beauty with their ray.
Then, too, the pearl from out the shell,
Unsightly in the sunless sea
(As 'twere a spirit forced to dwell
In form unlovely), was set free,
And round the neck of woman threw
A light it lent, and borrow'd too.

                              MOORE.

Fig—Argument.

September 17.

. . . . "It is in vain,
I see, to argue against the grain;
Or, like the stars, incline men to
What they're averse themselves to do;
For when disputes are wearied out,
'Tis interest still resolves the doubt:
A man convinced against his will,
Is of the same opinion still.

BUTLER.

Chrysanthemum—Cheerfulness.

September 18.

Let's take this world as some wide scene,
  Through which, in frail but buoyant boat,
With skies now dark, and now serene,
  Together thou and I must float.

. . . .

Should chilling winds and rains come on,
  We'll raise our awning 'gainst the shower,
Sit closer till the storm is gone,
  And smiling wait a sunnier hour.

And if that sunnier hour should shine,
  We'll know its brightness cannot stay;
But, happy while 'tis mine and thine,
  Complain not when it fades away.

MOORE.

Flax—Domestic Virtues.

September 19.

Around each pure domestic shrine
Bright flowers of Eden bloom and twine,
  Our hearths are altars all;
The prayers of hungry souls and poor,
Like armèd angels at the door,
  Our unseen foes appal.

KEBLE

September 20.

Hop—Injustice.

. . . .
Such ones ill judge of love, that cannot
    love,
Ne in their frozen hearts feele kindly flame;
Forthy they ought not thing unknowne re-
    prove,
Ne naturall affection faultlesse blame,
For fault of few that have abused the same;
For it of honor and all vertue is
The roote, and brings forth glorious flowres
    of fame,
That crowne true lovers with immortall
    bliss,
The meed of them that love, and do not
    love amisse.   SPENSER.

September 21.

Fuchsia—Taste.

What, then, is taste, but these internal
    powers,
Active and strong, and feelingly alive
To each fine impulse?—a discerning sense
Of decent and sublime, with quick disgust
From things deformed, or disarranged, or
    gross
In species? This no gems or stores of
    gold,
Nor purple state, nor culture can bestow,
But God alone, when first His active hand
Imprints the secret bias of the soul.
          AKENSIDE.

September 22.

Juniper—Protection.

When any, favour'd of high Jove,
Chance to pass through this advent'rous
    glade,
Swift as the sparkle of a glancing star,
I shoot from heaven, to give him safe
    convoy.

        MILTON.

Hydrangea—Boastfulness.

September 23.

. . . . AND here let those
Who boast in mortal things, and wonder-
ing tell
Of Babel and the works of Memphian
kings,
Learn how their greatest monuments of
fame,
And strength, and art, are easily outdone
By spirits reprobate; and in an hour,
What in an age they, with incessant toil
And hands innumerable, scarce perform.

MILTON.

**Indian Corn—
Eclat, or Triumph.**

September 24.

"TO-MORROW your Dictator
    Shall bring in triumph home
The spoils of thirty cities,
    To deck the shrines of Rome!"
Then burst from that great concourse
    A shout that shook the towers;
And some ran north, and some ran south,
    Crying, "The day is ours!"

MACAULAY

Lavender—Distrust.

September 25.

So, you think you love me, do you?
    Well, it may be so;
But there are many ways of loving,
    I have learnt to know:
Many ways, and but one true way,
    Which is very rare;
And the counterfeits look brightest,
    Though they will not wear.

ADELAIDE PROCTER.

September 26.

SACRED I'll hold the sacred name of wife,
And love thee to the sunset verge of life;
Yea, shall so much of empire o'er man's
    soul
Live in a wanton's smile, and no control
Bind down his heart to keep a steadier
    faith
For links that are to last from life to death?
Let those who can in transient loves re-
    joice—
Still to new hopes breathe forth successive
    sighs;
Give me the music of the accustom'd voice,
And the sweet light of long familiar eyes.

HON. MRS. NORTON.

Linden—Conjugal Love.

Love-lies-Bleeding—
Hopeless.

September 27

FAIR Hope is dead, and light
    Is quench'd in night.
What sound can break the silence of
    despair?
    O doubting heart!
    Thy sky is overcast,
    Yet stars shall rise at last,
    Brighter for darkness past,
And angels' silver voices stir the air.

ADELAIDE PROCTER.

Maize—Plenty.

September 28.

EARTH's increase and foison, plenty,
Barns and garners never empty;
Vines with clust'ring bunches growing,
Plants with goodly burden bowing;
Spring come to you at the farthest,
In the very end of harvest;
Scarcity and want shall shun you,
Ceres' blessing so is on you.

SHAKSPEARE.

**Michaelmas Daisy—
Afterthought.**

September 29.

"BELOVED Ruth!"—no more he said;
The wakeful Ruth at midnight shed
    A solitary tear:
She thought again—and did agree
With him to sail across the sea,
    And drive the flying deer.

                WORDSWORTH.

September 30.

Walnut—Stratagem.

O, you who have the charge of Love,
    Keep him in rosy bondage bound,
As, in the fields of bliss above,
    He sits, with flow'rets fetter'd round;
Loose not a tie that round him clings,
    Nor ever let him use his wings;
For ev'n an hour, a minute's flight,
    Will rob the plumes of half their light;
Like that celestial bird, whose nest
    Is found beneath far Eastern skies,
Whose wings, though radiant when at rest,
    Lose all their glory when he flies.

                MOORE.

Pine-apple—Perfection.

October 1.

To gild refinèd gold, to paint the lily,
To throw a perfume on the violet;
To smooth the ice, or add another hue
Unto the rainbow, or with taper light
To seek the beauteous eye of Heaven to
    garnish,—
Is wasteful and ridiculous excess.

              SHAKSPEARE.

October 2.

. . . THE slightest feeling, stirr'd
   By trivial fancy, seek
Expression in that golden word,
   They tarnish while they speak.

Nay, let the heart's slow, rare decree
   That word in reverence keep;
Silence herself should only be
   More sacred and more deep.

        ADELAIDE PROCTER.

Red Chrysanthemum—Love.

October 3.

WHAT is Genius? 'tis a flame
Kindling all the human frame;
'Tis a ray that lights the eye,
Soft in love, in battle high :
'Tis the lightning of the mind,
Unsubdued and undefined ;
'Tis the flood that pours along
The full, clear melody of song ;
'Tis the sacred boon of Heaven,
To its choicest favourites given.
They who feel, can paint it well :
What is Genius?—Byron, tell !

        PERCIVAL.

Plane Tree—Genius.

October 4.

. . . . HIS present mind
Was under fascination ; he beheld
A vision, and adored the thing he saw.
Arabian fiction never fill'd the world
With half the wonders that were wrought
    for him.
Earth breathed in one great presence of
    the Spring ;
Life turned the meanest of her implements,
Before his eyes, to price above all gold.
The house she dwelt in was a sainted
    shrine,
Her chamber window did surpass in glory
The portals of the dawn ; all Paradise
Could, by the simple opening of a door,
Let itself in upon him.

        WORDSWORTH.

Honesty—Fascination.

**Pomegranate Blossom—
A Warning.**

Azalea—Adoration.

**Hollyhock—
Female Ambition.**

October 5.

TREASURE Love, though ready
  Still to live without;
In your fondest trust, keep
  Just *one* thread of doubt.

Build on no to-morrow,
  Love has but to-day;
If the links seem slackening,
  Cut the bond away.

Trust no prayer or promise;
  Words are grains of sand:
To keep your heart unbroken,
  Hold it in your hand.
ADELAIDE PROCTER.

October 6.

NOR was it long ere by her side
I found myself whole happy days.
 . . . .

Though gross the air on earth I drew,
'Twas blessèd while she breathed it too:
Though dark the flowers, though dim the
  sky,
Love lent them light while she was nigh.
Throughout creation, I but knew
Two separate worlds,—the *one*, that small
  Beloved and consecrated spot,
Where Lea *was*; the *other*, all
  The dull, wide waste, where she was *not*.
MOORE.

October 7.

LOVE, that of every woman's heart
Will have the whole, and not a part;
That is to her, in Nature's plan,
More than ambition to a man,—
Her light, her life, her very breath,
With no alternative but death!
LONGFELLOW.

October 8.

CLAMOUR grew dumb, unheard was shep-
　　herd's song,
And silence girt the woods; no warbling
　　tongue
Talk'd to the echo; satyrs broke their
　　dance,
And all the upper world lay in a trance.
Only the curlèd streams soft chidings
　　kept;
And little gales, that from the green leaf
　　swept
Dry summer's dust, in fearful whisperings
　　stirr'd,
As loth to waken any singing bird,
　　　　　　　　　　　　　BROWNE.

Belladonna—Silence.

Myrtle—Love.

October 9.

(To the Evening Star.)

O, SACRED to the fall of day,
　　Queen of propitious stars, appear!
And early rise, and long delay,
　　When Caroline herself is here!

. . . .

Thus, ever thus, at day's decline,
　　In converse sweet, to wander far;
O, bring with thee my Caroline,
　　And thou shalt be my ruling star!
　　　　　　　　　　　　CAMPBELL.

Oak Leaf—Valour.

October 10.

FEAR to do base, unworthy things, is
　　valour;
If they be done to us, to suffer them,
Is valour too.
　　　　　　　　　　BEN JONSON.

Nasturtium—Patriotism.

October 11.

But where to find that happiest spot below,
Who can direct, when all pretend to know?
The shuddering tenant of the frigid zone
Boldly proclaims the happiest spot his own,
Extols the treasures of his stormy seas,
And his long nights of revelry and ease:
The naked negro, panting at the line,
Boasts of his golden sands and palmy wine,
Basks in the glare, or stems the tepid wave,
And thanks his gods for all the good they
    gave.
Such is the patriot's boast; where'er we
    roam,
His first, best country ever is at home.
                GOLDSMITH.

Black Pine—Pity.

October 12.

Upon my heart thy accents sweet,
    Of peace and pity, fell like dew
On flowers half dead; thy lips did meet
    Mine tremblingly; thy dark eyes threw
Their soft persuasion on my brain,
Charming away its dream of pain.
                SHELLEY.

**Wild Plum Tree—
Independence.**

October 13.

Thy spirit, Independence, let me share,
    Lord of the lion heart and eagle eye!
Thy steps I follow, with my bosom bare,
    Nor heed the storm that howls along
      the sky.
                SMOLLETT.

October 14.

The soul's dark cottage, battered and decayed,
Lets in new light through chinks that time has made;
Stronger by weakness, wiser, men become,
As they draw near to their eternal home:
Leaving the old, both worlds at once they view,
That stand upon the threshold of the new.

WALLER.

Snowberry Tree—Age.

October 15.

Oh! Nanny, wilt thou go with me,
    Nor sigh to leave the flaunting town?
Can silent glens have charms for thee,
    The lowly cot, and russet gown?
No longer drest in silken sheen,
    No longer deck'd with jewels rare,—
Say, canst thou quit each courtly scene,
    Where thou wert fairest of the fair?

PERCY.

Everlasting Pea—
"Wilt thou go with me?"

October 16.

Hark! where the martial trumpet fills the air;
How the roused multitude come round to stare!
Sport drops his ball, Toil throws his hammer by,
Thrift breaks a bargain off to please his eye.
Up fly the windows; ev'n fair Mistress Cook,
Though dinner burn, must run to take a look.

SPRAGUE.

Sycamore – Curiosity.

Thistle—Austerity

October 17.

WE need not bid, for cloister'd cell,
Our neighbour and our work farewell,
Nor strive to wind ourselves too high
For sinful man beneath the sky.

The trivial round, the common task,
Would furnish all we ought to ask :
Room to deny ourselves—a road
To bring us daily nearer God.

KEBLE

**Valerian—
Accommodating Disposition.**

October 18.

OH ! blest with temper, whose unchanging ray

Can make to-morrow cheerful as to-day ;

She who can love a sister's charms, and hear

Sighs for a daughter with unwounded ear ;

She who ne'er answers till her husband cools,

And if she rules him, never shows she rules ;

Charms by accepting, by submitting, sways,

And has her humour most, when she obeys.

POPE.

**Tall Sunflower—
Haughtiness.**

October 19.

IN vain all the knights of the Underwald woo'd her ;

Though brightest of maidens, the proudest was she :

Brave chieftains they sought her, and young minstrels they sued her ;

But worthy were none of the high-born ladye.

MOORE.

October 20.

The mask is off—the charm is wrought--
And Selim to his heart has caught,
In blushes more than ever bright,
His Nourmahal, his Haram's Light.
And well do vanish'd frowns enhance
The charm of every brighten'd glance ;
And dearer seems each dawning smile,
For having lost its light awhile :
And happier now for all her sighs,
As on his arm her head reposes,
She whispers him, with laughing eyes,
    " Remember, love, the Feast of Roses !"
                            MOORE.

Hazel—Reconciliation.

October 21.

Drink to me only with thine eyes,
    And I will pledge with mine ;
Or leave a kiss within the cup,
    And I'll not ask for wine.
The thirst that from the soul doth rise,
    Doth ask a drink divine :
But might I of Love's nectar sip,
    I would not change for thine.
                            BEN JONSON.

Vine—Intoxication.

October 22.

The foam-fringe at their feet was not more
    white
Than her pale cheeks, as, downcast, she
    replied :
No, Godfrid, no !   Farewell—farewell !
    You might
Have been my star : a star fell once by
    pride.
But since you furl your wings and veil
    your light,
I cling to Mary, and Christ crucified !
Leave me—nay, leave me, ere it be too late ;
Better part here, than part at heaven's
    gate !"   ALFRED AUSTIN.

Spruce Pine—Farewell.

**Canary Grass—
Perseverance.**

October 23.

PERSEVERANCE is a virtue
That wins each god-like act, and plucks
  success
E'en from the spear-proof crest of rugged
  danger.

WILLIAM HAVARD.

**White Chrysanthemum—
Truth.**

October 24.

BEFORE thy mystic altar, heavenly Truth,
I kneel in manhood, as I knelt in youth :
Thus let me kneel, till this dull form decay
And life's last shade be brighten'd by thy
  ray :
Then shall my soul, now lost in clouds be-
  low,
Soar without bound, without consuming
  glow

SIR WILLIAM JONES.

Myrrh—Gladness.

October 25.

ALL my error, all my weakness,
  All my vain delusions fled ;
Hope again revived, and gladness
  Waved its wings above my head.

Like the wanderer of the desert,
  When across the weary sand
Breathes the perfume from the thickets
  Bordering on the promised land.

AYTOUN.

October 26.

Wild Geranium—
Steadfast Piety.

OLD friends, old scenes, will lovelier be,
As more of Heaven in each we see ;
Some softening gleam of love and prayer
Shall dawn on every cross and care.

As for some dear familiar strain
Untired we ask, and ask again,
Ever, in its melodious store,
Finding a spell unheard before ;—

Such is the bliss of souls serene,
When they have sworn, and steadfast
    mean,
Counting the cost, in all t' espy
Their God, in all themselves deny.

KEBLE.

October 27.

Chesnut—Luxury.

SANGUINE he was, and studied pleasure
    most ;
His morning's draught, sack, with a nut-
    brown toast.
All delicates that money could procure
He had—a nice, luxurious epicure.

POPE'S "CHAUCER."

October 28.

Purple Columbine—
Resolution.

LET come what will, I mean to bear it out.
And either live with glorious Victory,
Or die with Fame, renown'd in chivalry.
He is not worthy of the honeycomb,
That shuns the hive because the bees have
    stings.

SHAKSPEARE.

109

Dock—Patience.

October 29.

WAIT; yet I do not tell you
　　The hour you long for now
Will not come with its radiance vanish'd
　　And a shadow upon its brow.

Yet far through the misty future,
　　With a crown of starry light,
An hour of joy you know not,
　　Is winging her silent flight.

ADELAIDE PROCTER.

**Night=scented Stock—
Devotion.**

October 30.

Go when the morning shineth,
　　Go when the moon is bright
Go when the eve declineth,
　　Go in the hush of night;
Go with pure mind and feeling,
　　Fling every fear away,
And in thy chamber kneeling,
　　Do thou in secret pray.

BELL.

**Slighted Love—
Yellow Chrysanthemum.**

October 31.

WHEN I sang of Ariadne,
　　Sang the old and mournful tale,
How her faithless lover, Theseus,
　　Left her to lament and wail;—

Then thy eyes would fill and glisten,
　　Her complaint could soften thee;
Thou hast wept for Ariadne—
　　Theseus' self might weep for me!

AYTOUN

November 1.

The fine and noble way to kill a foe,
  Is not to kill him; you with kindness may
So change him, that he shall cease to be so,
  And then he's slain: Sigismund used to
    say,
His pardons put his foes to death; for when
He mortified their hate, he kill'd them then.

ALEYN.

Burr—Kindness.

November 2.

But, O, the heavy change now thou art
    gone!—
Now thou art gone, and never must re-
    turn!
Thee, Shepherd, thee, the woods and desert
    caves,
With wild thyme and the gadding vine
    o'ergrown,
And all their echoes mourn;
The willows, and the hazel copses green,
Shall now no more be seen
Fanning their joyous leaves to thy soft lays.
As killing as the canker to the rose,
Or taint-worm to the weanling herds that
    graze,
Or frost to flowers that their gay wardrobe
    wear,
When first the white-thorn blows:
Such, Lycidas, thy loss to shepherd's ear.

MILTON.

Aspen—Lamentation.

November 3.

How charming is divine Philosophy!
Not harsh and crabbed, as dull fools sup-
    pose,
But musical as is Apollo's lute,
And a perpetual feast of nectar'd sweets,
Where no crude surfeit reigns.

MILTON.

Pitch Pine—Philosophy.

III

Cranberry—
Cure for Heartache.

November 4.

I KNOW where the winged visions dwell,
   That around the night-bed play;
I know each herb and flow'rets bell,
   Where they hide their wings by day.

. . . .

The dream of the injured, patient mind,
   That smiles with the wrongs of men,
Is found in the bruised and wounded rind
   Of the cinnamon, sweetest then.
      Then hasten we, maid,
      To twine our braid ;
To-morrow the dreams and flow'rs will fade.
                 MOORE.

Hemp—Fate.

November 5.

FULL half an hour to-day I tried my lot,
   With various flowers, and every one still
      said,
" She loves me "—" Loves me not ! "
And if this meant a vision long since fled—
If it meant fortune, fame, or peace of
   thought—
If it meant——but I dread
To speak what you may know so well :
Still there was truth in that sad oracle.
                SHELLEY.

Globe Amaranth—
Unchangeable.

November 6.

IT will live, no eyes will see it ;
   In my soul it will lie deep,
Hidden from all ; but I shall feel it
   Often stirring in my sleep.

So remember, that the friendship
   Which you now think poor and vain,
Will endure in hope and patience,
   Till you ask for it again.
           ADELAIDE PROCTER.

November 7.

But let my due feet never fail
To walk the studious cloister's pale,
And love the high embowed roof,
With antic pillars massy proof,
And storied windows richly dight,
Casting a dim religious light,
There let the pealing organ blow,
To the full-voiced quire below,
In service high, and anthem clear,
As may with sweetness, through mine ear,
Dissolve me into ecstasies,
And bring all heaven before my eyes.

MILTON.

Snow Berry.—
Thoughts of Heaven.

November 8.

Spirit, who sweepest the wild harp of
    Time !
It is most hard, with an untroubled ear,
Thy dark inwoven harmonies to hear !
Yet, mine eye fix'd on heaven's unchanging
    clime,
Long when I listen'd, free from mortal fear,
With inward stillness, and submitted mind :
When, lo ! its folds far waving on the wind,
I saw the train of the departing year !
    Starting from my silent sadness,
    Then, with no unholy madness,
Ere yet the entered cloud foreclosed my
    sight,
I raised the impetuous song, and solemnised
    his flight !

COLERIDGE.

White Poplar—Time.

November 9.

. . . . May he live
Longer than I have time to tell his years !
Ever beloved, and loving may his rule be ;
And, when old Time shall lead him to his
    end,
Goodness and he fill up one monument !

SHAKSPEARE.

Ash Tree—Grandeur.

Bay Leaf—Faithfulness.

November 10.

PERHAPS in some long twilight hour,
  Like those we have known of old,
When past shadows gather round you,
  And your present friends grow cold;

You may stretch your hands out towards
  me,
  Ah! you will—I know not when——
I shall nurse my love, and keep it
  Faithfully for you till then.

ADELAIDE PROCTER.

November 11.

Bilberry—Treachery.

EYES, eyes, that were so lovely, shall I see
  your glance no more?
Heart, heart, that was so tender, will your
  grief for me be sore?—
And none be near to warn thee, when he
  breathes his treacherous vow,
That he slew thine own true lover, who
  vainly calls thee now,
And murmurs, "Helen! Helen!" with the
  death damp on his brow!
For my friend gave me false counsel, that
  I might die, and he might live;
For dear, dear, dear's the love that Helen
  Douglas has to give.

HON. MRS. NORTON.

November 12.

Bindweed—Profuseness.

HEAVEN hath its crown of stars, the earth
  Her glory robe of flowers,—
The sea its gems, the grand old woods
  Their songs and greening showers:
The birds have homes, where leaves and
  blooms
  In beauty wreathe above;
High yearning hearts their rainbow dreams
  And we, sweet—we have love!

MASSEY.

November 13.

SHALL I be left forgotten in the dust,
  When Fate, relenting, lets the flower
    revive?
Shall Nature's voice, to man alone unjust,
  Bid him, though doom'd to perish, hope
    to live?
Is it for this fair Virtue oft must strive
  With disappointment, penury, and pain?
No: Heaven's immortal spring shall yet
    arrive,
  And man's majestic beauty bloom again,
Bright through the eternal year of Love's
    triumphant reign.

BEATTIE.

Cedar of Lebanon—
Incorruptibility.

November 14.

. . . .
A VIOLET by a mossy stone,
  Half hidden from the eye,—
Fair as a star, when only one
  Is shining in the sky:

She lived unknown, and few could know
  When Lucy ceased to be;
But she is in her grave, and, oh!
  The difference to me!

WORDSWORTH.

Bramble—Lowliness.

November 15.

GOLDEN sparkles, flashing gem,
  Lit the robes of each of them;
Cloak of velvet, robe of silk,
  Mantle snowy-white as milk;
Ring upon our bridle hand,
  Jewels on our belt and band;
Bells upon our golden reins,
  Tinkling spurs, and shining chains,—
In such merry mob we went,
  Riding to the tournament.

THORNBURY.

Red Salvia—Pomp.

115

Variegated Ivy—Brightness.

November 16.

Oh ! the light of life that sparkled
   In those bright and bounteous eyes !
Oh ! the blush of happy beauty,
   Tell-tale of the heart's surprise !
Oh ! the radiant light that girdled
   Field and forest, land and sea,
When we all were young together,
   And the earth was new to me.

AYTOUN.

November 17.

Cudweed—Remembrance.

Yet whenever I cross the river,
   On its bridge with wooden piers,
Like the odour of brine from the ocean,
   Comes the thought of other years.

And for ever, and for ever,
   As long as the river flows,—
As long as the heart has passions,
   As long as life has woes ;—

The moon and its broken reflection,
   And its shadows shall appear,
As the symbol of Love in heaven,
   And its wavering image here.

LONGFELLOW.

November 18.

Fern Moss—Content.

Divine Content !
  O ! could the world resent,
How much of bliss doth lie
  Wrapp'd up in thy
Delicious name ; and at
  How low a rate
Thou might'st be bought !
  No trade would driven be,
To purchase any wealth, but only thee.

BEAUMONT.

November 19.

How canst thou dream of Beauty as a thing
On which depends the heart's own wither-
    ing?
Lips budding red, with tints of vernal years,
And delicate lids of eyes that shed no tears,
And light that falls upon the shining hair,
As though it found a secret sunbeam there,—
These must go by, my Gertrude, must go by;
The leaf must wither, and the flower must
    die;
The rose can only have a rose's bloom:
Age would have wrought thy wondrous
    beauty's doom.

           HON. MRS. NORTON.

Parti-coloured Daisy—
Beauty.

November 20.

But where is Harold? Shall I then forget
To urge the gloomy wanderer o'er the wave?
Little reck'd he of all that men regret;
No loved one now in feign'd lament could
    rave;
No friend the parting hand extended gave,
Ere the cold stranger pass'd to other climes;
Hard in his heart, whom charms may not
    enslave;
But Harold felt not as in other times,
And left without a sigh the land of war and
    crimes.   BYRON.

Ebony—"You are hard.'

November 21.

Methinks I see thee stand, with pallid
    cheeks,
By Fra Hilario in his diocese;
As up the convent walls, in golden streaks
The ascending sunbeams mark the day's
    decrease;
And as he asks what there the stranger
    seeks,
Thy voice along the cloister whispers—
    Peace!   LONGFELLOW.

Gardinea—Peace.

November 22.

Black Prince Geranium—
Delusive Hopes.

Oh! ever thus, from childhood's hour,
  I've seen my fondest hopes decay;
I never loved a tree or flower,
  But 'twas the first to fade away.

I never nurst a dear gazelle,
  To glad me with its soft brown eye,
But when it came to know me well,
  And love me, it was sure to die.

MOORE.

November 23.

Sorrel—Parental Affection.

Ah, God! my child! my first, my living
    child!
I have been dreaming of a thing like thee,
Ere since, a babe, upon the mountains wild,
I nursed my mimic babe upon my knee.
In girlhood I had visions of thee; Love
Came to my riper youth, and still I clove
Unto thine image, born within my brain,
So like, as even there thy germ had lain!
My blood! my voice! my thought! my
    dream achieved!
Oh! till this double life, I had not lived!

WADE.

November 24.

Goat's Rue—Reason.

Dim as the borrow'd beams of moon and
    stars,
To lone, weary, wandering travellers,
Is Reason to the soul; and as on high
Those rolling fires discover but the sky,
Not light us here, so Reason's glimmering
    ray
Was lent, not to assure our doubtful way,
But guide us upward to a better day.
And as those nightly tapers disappear,
When day's bright lord ascends our hemi-
    sphere;
So pale grows Reason at Religion's sight,
So dies, and so dissolves, in supernatural
    light.

DRYDEN.

November 25.

THERE is no dearth of kindness
    In this world of ours,
Only in our blindness
    We gather thorns for flowers!

Outward we are spurning,
    Trampling one another,
While we are inly yearning
    At the name of brother.
MASSEY.

Fir of Gilead—Kindness.

November 26.

ARE there not aspirations in each heart,
    After a better, brighter world than this?
Longings for beings nobler in each part,
    Things more exalted, steep'd in deeper
        bliss?
Who gave us these? what are they? Soul,
    in thee
The bud is budding now for Immortality!
NICOLL.

Pine Branch—Aspiration.

November 27.

The might of one fair face sublimes my
    love,
For it hath wean'd my heart from low de-
    sires ;
Nor death I heed, nor purgatory fires :
Thy beauty, antepast of joys above,
Instructs me in the bliss that saints approve :
For, oh ! how good, how beautiful must be
The God that made so good a thing as thee,
So fair an image of the Heavenly Dove !
Forgive me if I cannot turn away
From those sweet eyes, that are my earthly
    heaven ;
For they are guiding stars, benignly given,
To tempt my footsteps to the upward way ;
And if I dwell too fondly in thy sight,
I live and love in God's peculiar light.
MICHAEL ANGELO.

Variegated Geranium—
Charms of Women.

Helenium—Tears.

November 28.

How lovely in her tears!
What beams her beauty darts through
    clouds of woe!
So Venus look'd, when, wet with silver
    drops,
Above the floods she raised her shining
    head,
Gilded the waves, and charm'd the won-
    dering gods.

OWEN.

Czar Violet—
Kindness and Worth.

November 29.

AND never brooch the folds combined,
Above a heart more good and kind:
Her kindness and her worth to spy,
You need but gaze on Ellen's eye.
Not Katrine, in her mirror blue,
Gives back the shaggy banks more true,
Than every free-born glance confess'd
The guileless movements of her breast.

SCOTT.

Fuller's Thistle—
Misanthropy.

November 30.

AND dost thou ask what secret woe
    I bear, corroding joy and youth?
And wilt thou vainly seek to know
    A pang, ev'n thou must fail to soothe?

It is not love, it is not hate,
    Nor low Ambition's honours lost,
That bids me loathe my present state,
    And fly from all I prized the most.

It is that weariness that springs
    From all I meet, or hear, or see;
To me no pleasure beauty brings,
    Thine eyes have scarce a charm for me

BYRON.

December 1.

THERE be none of Beauty's daughters
  With a magic like thee;
And like music on the waters
  Is thy sweet voice to me:
When, as if its sound were causing
The charmèd ocean's pausing,
The waves lie still and gleaming,
And the lull'd winds seem dreaming,
  And the midnight moon is weaving
  Her bright chain o'er the deep,
Whose breast is gently heaving,
  As an infant's asleep:
So the spirit bows before thee,
To listen and adore thee,
With a full but soft emotion,
Like the swell of summer's ocean.

BYRON.

December 2.

I SHALL know by the gleam and glitter
  Of the golden chain you wear—
By your heart's calm strength in loving,
  Of the fire they have had to bear.

Beat on, true heart, for ever;
  Shine bright, strong golden chain,
And bless the cleansing fire,
  And the furnace of living pain.

ADELAIDE PROCTER.

December 3.

No single virtue we could most commend,
Whether the wife, the mother, or the friend:
For she was all, in that supreme degree,
That as no one prevail'd, so all was she.
The several parts lay hidden in the piece,
The occasion but exerted that or this.
A wife as tender, and as true withal,
As the first woman was, before her fall;
Made for the man, of whom she was a part,
Made to attract his eyes, and keep his heart.

DRYDEN.

Scotch Thistle—Retaliation.

December 4.

LEARN from yon orient shell to love thy
    foe,
And store with pearls the hand that brings
    thee woe;
Free, like yon rock, from base vindictive
    pride,
Emblaze with gems the wrist that tears
    thy side.
With fruit nectareous, or balmy flower,
All Nature calls aloud, "Shall man do less,
Than heal the smiter, and the railer bless?"

HAFIZ.

Withered Leaves—
Melancholy.

December 5.

YES, the year is growing old,
    And his eye is pale and blear'd;
Death, with frosty hand and cold,
    Plucks the old man by the beard—
        Sorely, sorely!

The leaves are falling, falling,
    Solemnly and slow;
Caw, caw! the rooks are calling:
        It is a sound of woe—
        A sound of woe!

LONGFELLOW.

Hibiscus—Change.

December 6.

AND when to me you first made suit,
    How fair I was, you oft would say,
And, proud of conquest, pluck'd the fruit,
    Then left the blossom to decay.

Then, Earl, why didst thou leave the beds,
    Where roses and where lilies vie,
To seek a primrose, whose pale shades
    Must sicken when those gauds are by?

MICKLE.

December 7.

Lint—Obligation.

DUTY, like a strict preceptor,
  Sometimes frowns, or seems to frown;
Choose her thistle for thy sceptre,
  While youth's roses are thy crown.

Grasp it: if thou shrink and tremble.
  Fairest damsel of the green,
Thou wilt lack the only symbol
  That proclaims a genuine Queen.

WORDSWORTH.

December 8.

Osmunda—Dreams.

AND dreams in their development have
      breath;
And tears, and tortures, and the touch of
      joy;
They leaves a weight upon our waking
      thoughts,
They take a weight from off our waking
      toils:
They do divide our being; they become
A portion of ourselves, as of our time,
And look like heralds of eternity.
They pass like spirits of the past; they
      speak
Like sibyls of the future; they have power,
The tyranny of pleasure and of pain.

BYRON.

December 9.

Lemon—Piquancy.

PINS she sticks into my shoulder,
  Places needles in my chair;
And when I begin to scold her,
  Tosses back her combèd hair,
  With so saucy, vex'd an air,
That the pitying beholder
Cannot brook that I should scold her;
Then again she comes, and bolder,
  Blacks again this face of mine.

BON GAULTIER.

123

American Ivy—
Strong Friendship.

Lignum Vitæ—Homage.

Broken Straws—Division.

December 10.

For we were nursed upon the selfsame
    hill,
Fed the same flock by fountain, shade,
    and rill;
Together both, ere the high lawns appear'd.
Under the opening eyelids of the morn,
We drove a-field, and both together heard
What time the gray-fly winds her sultry
    horn;
Batt'ning our flocks with the fresh dews of
    night,
Oft till the star that rose at evening, bright
Toward heaven's descent had sloped his
    west'ring wheel.

MILTON.

December 11.

And I watch'd thee ever fondly—
    Watch'd thee, dearest, from afar,
With the mute and humble homage
    Of the Indian to a star.

AYTOUN.

December 12.

And ruder words will soon rush in,
To spread the breach that words begin,
And eyes forget the gentle ray
They wore in courtship's smiling day;
And voices lose the tone that shed
A tenderness round all they said;
Till fast declining, one by one,
The sweetnesses of love are gone,
And hearts, so lately mingled, seem
Like broken clouds, or like the stream
That smiling left the mountain's brow,
    As though its water ne'er could sever,
Yet, ere it reach'd the plain below,
    Breaks into floods that part for ever.

MOORE.

December 13.

Is thy cruse of comfort failing?—rise, and
    share it with another,
And through all the years of famine, it
    shall serve thee and thy brother.
Love Divine will fill the storehouse, and
    thy handful still renew:
Scanty fare for one, will often make a
    royal feast for two.
For the heart grows rich in giving; all its
    wealth is living gain:
Seeds, which mildew in the garner, scat-
    tered, fill with gold the plain.

MRS. CHARLES.

Heps and Haws—
Compensation.

December 14.

Like as the culver on the barèd bough
Sits mourning for the absence of her
    mate,
And in her songs sends many a wishful
    vow
For his return, that seems to linger late;
So I, alone now left, disconsolate,
Mourn to myself the absence of my love,
And wandering here and there, all deso-
    late,
Seek with my plaints to match that
    mournful dove.

SPENSER.

Wormwood—Absence.

December 15.

Oh! why left I my hame?
    Why did I cross the deep?
Oh! why left I the land
    Where my forefathers sleep?
I sigh for Scotia's shore,
    And I gaze across the sea;
But I canna get a blink
    O' my ain countrie.

GILFILLAN.

Hothouse Heath – Exile.

Scotch Fir—Perseverance in Pursuit of Knowledge.

December 16.

WHAT is earthly victory? Press on!
For it hath tempted angels—yet press on!
For it shall make you mighty among men,
And from the eyrie of your eagle thought
Ye shall look down on monarchs—O, press
    on!
For the high ones, and powerful, shall come
To do you reverence; and the beautiful
Will know the purer language of your brow
And read it like a talisman of love.
Press on! for it is godlike to unloose
The spirit, and forget yourself in thought.

WILLIS.

Flowering Laurel—Goodness.

December 17.

THOUGH holy in himself, and virtuous,
He still to sinful men was mild and piteous;
Not of reproach imperious or malign,
But in his teaching soothing and benign.
To draw them on to heaven, by reason fair
And good example, was his daily care.
But were there one perverse and obstinate,
Were he of lofty or of low estate,
Him would he sharply with reproof astound:
A better priest is nowhere to be found.
He waited not on pomp or reverence,
Nor made himself a spicèd conscience.
The love of Christ and his apostles twelve
He taught; but first he followed it him-
    self.

CHAUCER.

Ivy Berry—Warning.

December 18.

I COME—and if I come in vain,
Never, oh! never we meet again!
Thou hast done a fearful deed,
In falling away from thy fathers' creed;
But dash that turban to earth, and sign
The sign of the cross, and for ever be mine;
Wring the black drop from thy heart,
And to-morrow unites us, no more to part.

BYRON.

December 19.

And may at last my weary age
Find out the peaceful hermitage,
The hairy gown, and mossy cell,
Where I may sit, and rightly spell
Of every star that heaven doth show,
And every herb that sips the dew ;
Till old experience do attain
To something like prophetic strain.

MILTON.

Moss—Seclusion.

December 20.

Who seeks a friend, should come disposed
To exhibit, in full bloom disclosed,
    The graces and the beauties
That form the character he seeks ;
But 'tis a union that bespeaks
    Reciprocated duties.

. . . .

But will sincerity suffice?
It is indeed above all price,
    And must be made the basis ;
But every virtue of the soul
Must constitute the charming whole,
    All shining in their places.

COWPER.

Fern—Sincerity.

December 21.

Alas ! how light a cause may move
Dissension between hearts that love —
Hearts that the world in vain had tried,
And sorrow had more closely tied ;
That stood the storm when waves were
    rough,
Yet in a sunny hour fall off ;
Like ships that have gone down at sea,
When heaven was all tranquillity !
A something light as air—a look—
    A word unkind, or wrongly taken,—
Oh ! love that tempests never shook,
    A breath, a touch like this, hath shaken.

MOORE.

Broken Stalks—Dissension.

Parsley—Feasting.

December 22.

The fire, with well-dried logs supplied,
Went roaring up the chimney wide;
The huge hall-table's oaken face,
Scrubb'd till it shone, the day to grace,
Bore then upon its massive board
No mark to part the squire and lord.
Then was brought in the lusty brawn,
By old blue-coated serving-man;
Then the grim boar's head frown'd on high
Crested with bays and rosemary.
. . . .
The wassail round, in good brown bowls
Garnish'd with ribbons, blithely trolls.
Then the huge sirloin reek'd; hard by,
Plum-porridge stood, and Christmas pie.

SCOTT.

Trefoil—Revenge.

December 23.

" BUT, oh! revenge is sweet!"—
Thus think the crowd, who, eager to engage,
Take quickly fire, and kindle into rage,
Not so mild Thales nor Chrysippus thought,
Nor that good man, who drank the poisonous draught,
With mind serene, and could not wish to see
His vile accuser drink so deep as he.
Exalted Socrates! divinely brave!
Injured he fell, and dying he forgave:
Too noble for revenge, which still we find
The weakest frailty of a feeble mind.

DRYDEN.

Holly Berry—Greeting.

December 24.

AND who but listen'd, till was paid
Respect to every inmate's claim;
The greeting given, the music played,
In honour of each household name,
Duly pronounced, with lusty call,
And merry Christmas wish'd to all.

WORDSWORTH.

December 25.

But He, her fears to cease,
  Sent down the meek-eyed Peace;
She, crown'd with olive green, came softly
    sliding
  Down through the turning sphere,
  His ready harbinger,
With turtle wing the amorous clouds divid-
    ing;
And waving wide her myrtle wand,
She strikes an universal peace through
    sea and land.

. . . .

  Peaceful was the night,
  Wherein the Prince of Light
His reign of peace upon the earth began:
  The winds with wonder whist,
  Smoothly the waters kist,
Whisp'ring new joys to the mild ocean,
Who now hath quite forgot to rave,
While birds of calm sit brooding on the
    charmèd wave.   MILTON.

December 26.

Power laid his rod of rule aside,
And Ceremony doff'd his pride.
The heir, with roses in his shoes,
That night might village partner choose:
The lords, underogating, share
The vulgar game of "Post and Pair."
All hail'd, with uncontroll'd delight
And general voice, the happy night,
That to the cottage, as the crown,
Brought tidings of salvation down.
    SCOTT.

Walnuts—Sociality.

December 27.

Order is Heaven's first law—a glorious
    law!
Seen in those pure and beauteous isles of
    light,
That come and go, as circling months fulfil
Their high behest; nor less on earth dis-
    cern'd,
'Mid rocks snow-clad, or wastes of herb-
    less sand;
Throughout all climes, beneath all varying
    skies,
Fixing for e'en the smallest flower that
    blooms,
Its place of growth.   MILTON.

Fir Cone—Order.

Holly—Foresight.

December 28.

"PROPHET," said I, "thing of evil !—prophet still, if bird or devil !
By that heaven that bends above us—by
that God we both adore—
Tell this soul with sorrow laden, if, within
the distant Aïdenn,
It shall clasp a sainted maiden, whom the
angels name Lenore—
Clasp a rare and radiant maiden, whom
the angels name Lenore ?"
    Quoth the Raven, "Never more !"
                                EDGAR POE.

Christmas Rose—
"Tranquillize my anxiety.'

December 29.

THOUGH the doom of swift decay
    Shocks the soul, where life is strong.—
Though, for frailer hearts, the day
    Lingers sad and overlong ;—
Still the weight will find a leaven,
    Still the spoiler's hand is slow,
While the future has its Heaven,
    And the past, its long ago.
                        LORD HOUGHTON,

Ashen Faggot—Festivity.

December 30.

THEN came the merry maskers in,
And carols roar'd with blithesome din ;
If unmelodious was the song,
It was a hearty note, and strong ;
Who lists, might in the mumming see
Traces of ancient mystery.
White shirts supplied the masquerade,
And smutted cheeks the visors made ;
But, O ! what maskers richly dight
Can boast of bosoms half so light !
England was Merry England, when
Old Christmas brought his sports again.
                                SCOTT.

December 31.

ORPHAN hours, the year is dead :
 Come and sigh, come and weep !
Merry hours, smile instead,
 For the year is but asleep :
See, it smiles as it is sleeping,
Mocking your untimely weeping.

 . . . .

January grey is here,
 Like a sexton by her grave
February bears the bier,
 March with grief doth howl and rave ;
And April weeps—but, O ye hours !
Follow with May's fairest flowers.
SHELLEY.